"Hey, man, I don't want any trouble."

The kid turned and lost himself in the crowd. Royce saw the angry sparks in Heather's green eyes. She opened her mouth, but before she squawked a single protest, he snatched her arm and tugged her toward the exit. He made it as far as the door before she dug in her heels. It was either stop or drag her the rest of the way. He stopped.

"How dare—"

"Not now." He flung open the door. His hand firmly against her back, he propelled her out of the bar.

The waiter's eyes widened. "Problem, Mayor?"

"Problem's leaving." He followed Heather outside, grateful she hadn't put up a bigger fuss. He grinned at the outrage on her face.

Compared with her teen years, tonight's rescue had been relatively painless.

Dear Reader,

If there's one thing I dislike, it's someone telling me I can't do something. That's a surefire way to motivate me to prove that person wrong. In that respect, the heroine in this story is a lot like me.

Royce McKinnon, mayor of Nowhere, Texas, throws down the gauntlet when he tells Heather Henderson she doesn't have what it takes to run her deceased father's feed store.

Royce took Heather under his wing when her mother ran off, leaving a young Heather with a negligent alcoholic father. Heather admits she probably would have turned into a "statistic" if Royce hadn't kept her in line and in school. But she's all grown up now and doesn't want or need Royce's unsolicited advice.

Heather is *Homeward Bound,* not only determined to prove she's capable of managing an almost-bankrupt business, but also determined to uncover the deep, dark secret she suspects is the real reason Royce doesn't want her returning to Nowhere.

Sit back and enjoy the show as Heather challenges Royce's sanity with her feminine wiles and spunky spirit. Who can resist a small-town girl with an attitude!

I'm always happy to hear from readers. Please visit me at www.marinthomas.com.

Happy reading!

Marin

HOMEWARD BOUND

MARIN THOMAS

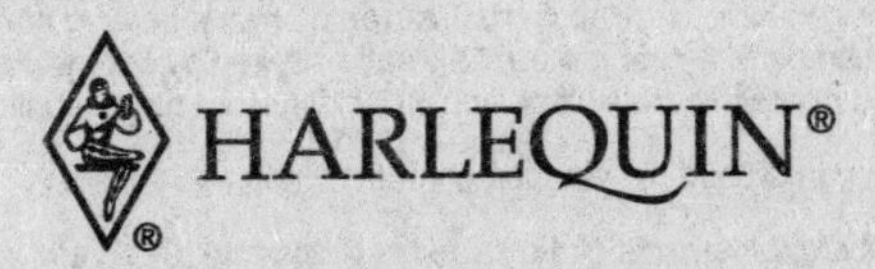

TORONTO • NEW YORK • LONDON
AMSTERDAM • PARIS • SYDNEY • HAMBURG
STOCKHOLM • ATHENS • TOKYO • MILAN • MADRID
PRAGUE • WARSAW • BUDAPEST • AUCKLAND

ISBN 0-373-75083-8

HOMEWARD BOUND

This edition published by arrangement with Harlequin Books S.A.

www.eHarlequin.com

Printed in U.S.A.

To my high school girlfriends from Janesville, Wisconsin—
Jenny, Lynn, Sue, Holly, Kay and Dana:

What a talented bunch of girls we were at Craig High School. We had brains, beauty, athletic talent, acting talent, singing talent, musical talent...and even a salutatorian among us. We've come a long way in our individual lives and careers. Through the years and across state lines we've manage to keep in touch. I treasure our friendships and feel blessed to have so many fond memories of our high school days together...well, except for the spring break trip to Sue's family cabin our senior year....

Books by Marin Thomas

HARLEQUIN AMERICAN ROMANCE

1024—THE COWBOY AND THE BRIDE
1050—DADDY BY CHOICE

Prologue

Smoke tendrils curled into the air above the burned wreckage of the single-wide trailer. The debris continued to smolder under the late-May sky, the scorched ruins contrasting starkly with the bold pink-and-rose Texas sunset. The stench of singed fabric, melted rubber and seared wood saturated the air.

"Sheriff thinks it was accidental."

Royce McKinnon shifted his attention from the yellow Caution tape strung around the rubble to his aging foreman, Luke. "Probably was."

"Bet my best whittlin' knife he drunk himself stupid, then passed out with a lit cigarette stuck in his craw."

"Wouldn't be the first time." Royce rubbed his brow, trying to ease the throb that had plagued him for the past hour. "As soon as the fire inspector gives the okay, I'll make arrangements to have the wreckage hauled off to the dump." The trailer fire was the first real catastrophe Royce had had to deal with since being elected the town mayor of Nowhere two years ago.

Luke shoved a wad of chew between his lip and gum. "You gonna call her tonight?"

"No." The *her* was Heather Henderson. Daughter of the

man who'd perished in the fire. Melvin Henderson had never been considered one of Nowhere's exemplary citizens. Royce had had his share of run-ins with the man over the years—not one of them pleasant.

He wondered how Heather would take the news of her father's death. On a scale of one to ten, Henderson had a negative number in the fatherhood department. Heather's mother had split years ago, leaving her thirteen-year-old daughter at the mercy of a drunk, mean ol' son of a bitch. In the end, Heather had had no one to care about her.

Except for you.

Royce had been nineteen when he'd stumbled upon the teen bawling her eyes out on the loading dock at the back of her father's feed store. The lost look on her face when she'd sobbed that her mother had run away and left her behind had shaken Royce more than he'd cared to admit at the time.

That afternoon he'd sympathized with Heather's grief as if it had been his own. He'd known all too well the feeling of being abandoned. Both his parents had died in a boating accident when he was a young boy. His childless aunt and uncle had taken him in but had treated him no better than one of the cow dogs. They'd given him shelter. Food. A place to sleep. And in return, he'd worked his butt off, learning how to raise cattle and work around a ranch—not an easy task for a boy who'd lived in Southern California near the ocean for his whole life.

He may not have had a storybook childhood full of warm fuzzies, but he'd had a home—which was more than some people got. His aunt and uncle had left him the ranch in their wills, and for that, Royce had forgiven them for not being the loving parents he'd wanted.

Twelve years ago, after witnessing the anguish in Heather's eyes, something inside Royce had reached out to the young girl. He'd sworn he'd do everything in his power to make sure she believed at least one person cared—Royce McKinnon. But the friendship he'd envisioned between them had never materialized. Heather had turned into a hellion and had rebuffed his offers of help and guidance.

Keeping her in line became a full-time job. Many days he'd considered washing his hands of her, but something had compelled him not to give up on the teen. He didn't need to pay a psychologist a hundred bucks a half hour to inform him that he'd turned the need to be cared for into a need to care for others. He glanced at Luke. "I'll drive down to College Station tomorrow." Maybe after the five-hour drive south, he'd figure out how to break the news to Heather.

"Where is she livin' these days?"

"I believe in a house near campus." Heather had moved several times from one apartment or rental house to another since enrolling at the University of Texas A&M seven years ago. "I'll check the return address on her Christmas card." Royce had kept every one of Heather's holiday cards in a shoe box on his bedroom closet shelf.

"Seem to recall her writin' that she was workin' at a day care."

Day care? Why hadn't Heather put that information in her card to him? *Maybe because the last time you paid her a visit, you did more than jump all over her for changing majors again and not finishing college yet.* He supposed changing majors more than once and holding down a job made graduating in four years next to impossible.

As if it had happened only yesterday, the last visit

flashed before his eyes. Heather at twenty-two had looked nothing like the gangly adolescent he'd remembered riding herd over. He'd never forget the sight of her in those hip-hugging short shorts and the strappy little top that had molded her full breasts and had shouted to him and every redblooded male within two miles of the campus that she was a desirable woman. For the first time, his body had reacted to her in a not-so-brotherly way, exciting him and scaring the hell out of him all at once.

He might have handled himself better if his attraction to her had been one-sided, but he'd caught the breathy sound that had escaped Heather's mouth when she'd opened the apartment door and discovered him on the stoop. He'd noticed the sparkle of awareness in the blue eyes that had roamed up and down his body.

After he'd entered her apartment, he couldn't stop staring at her. From her blond head to her pink-painted toenails, she'd mesmerized him. Gone had been any trace of the troublemaker teen he'd remembered. Flustered by his attraction to her, he'd started an argument about her taking forever to graduate. Then she'd done the most amazing thing—she'd kissed him. Her kiss had knocked the fight right out of him. To this day he could still remember the feel of her soft lips feathering across his. After he'd gotten over his initial shock, he'd kissed her right back. Again. And again. At least he'd come to his senses before they'd ended up in the bedroom.

After he left the university that day, he'd been determined to persuade Heather to return to Nowhere and spend the summer with him at the ranch. A small part of him had been convinced that what he'd felt for her had been more than just lust. But fate had foiled his plans, destroying any chance of a future with her. He'd found out the hard way that life sometimes plays dirty tricks on people.

In the end, Heather hadn't spent the summer in Nowhere, and he'd tried to forget about their one passionate encounter and move on with life. Throwing himself into ranch work had helped, but the exhausting physical labor hadn't been enough to chase the college coed from his thoughts. So he'd run for mayor, hoping the added responsibility would keep him too busy to ponder what might have been. For the most part, his plan had worked.

Until now. The trailer fire was another one of life's nasty little jokes. Ready or not, he'd have to face Heather and deliver the news of her father's death in person.

"Sure you don't want me to tell her?" A stream of tobacco juice shot out of the gap between Luke's front teeth.

Royce's chest tightened; he was so tempted to take the old man up on his offer. "Nope. After I speak with the fire inspector in the morning, I'll hit the road."

If there was any good to come out of Henderson's death, it was that once the man's estate was settled, his daughter would have no reason to return to Nowhere.

And Heather Henderson would finally be out of his life for good.

Chapter One

"Duck…duck…duck… Bobby, that's cheating. Sit on your bottom."

Heather pressed her lips together to keep from laughing at the disgruntled five-year-old's freckled face. As soon as he wiggled his rump back down on the campus daycare's blue-carpeted floor, she patted the next head.

"Duck…duck…" Her hand hovered over a bright pink bow on top of a mountain of blond curls. If she "goosed" Rebecca, freckle-face would throw a temper tantrum, and carrot-top, on the other side of Rebecca, would most likely stick his hand out and trip the little girl.

Tapping the bow, Heather moved on. "Duck…duck… *goose!*"

A quick pat on Tommy's head and Heather was off as fast as her knees would move. The kids loved her duck-duck-goose rule that adults play the game on their knees. She almost made it back to the empty spot, but Tommy's fingers grazed her shoulder. She toppled over and tugged the boy to the floor.

"Dog pile!" Brian yelled, jumping through the air.

Heather clenched her stomach muscles right before Brian's butt landed on her midsection. The hundred-perday situps she struggled through every morning at the campus gym paid off tenfold in this job. The other five children joined in and she ended up buried beneath bodies that smelled like peanut butter and jelly, laundry detergent and Play-Doh.

She wiggled her fingers against a pair of legs covered in pink tights and smiled when little Sonja, normally quiet and withdrawn, belly-laughed along with the rest of the preschoolers. The sound of rambunctious laugher warmed Heather's heart. She couldn't remember ever laughing with such abandon and glee as a child.

"Excuse me, Heather."

Peeking between the squirming bodies, Heather spotted her supervisor's mud-colored Easy Spirit shoes inches from her nose. "Yes, Mrs. Richards?"

"There's someone here to see you. Come along, children. Snack time."

One by one, the munchkins popped off Heather and dashed across the room. Feeling as if she'd narrowly survived a school of hungry piranhas, she lay sprawled on the carpet, her clothes in disarray and her ponytail smashed to one side. She turned her head—and spotted a large pair of worn cowboy boots.

Uh-oh.

Inch by inch, her gaze strolled up denim-clad legs, slowed across solid thighs, then came to a complete stop at a well-endowed…One hip shifted, jarring her attention upward, past the shiny silver belt buckle. Past the six pearl snaps on the sky-blue western shirt. Past a whisker-stubbled chin. Straight to his eyes. Eyes that stirred up memories of—

"Heather."

Sucking in a deep breath, she braved a smile.

Eyes dark as chunks of coal stared solemnly down at her from under the brim of a seen-better-days black Stetson.

So he was going to pretend they'd never shared glorious kisses three years ago. Okay, fine. She could pretend, too. "Hello, Royce."

Her self-appointed guardian angel glowered. She imagined any sensible women would take one look at his expression, which hinted at a not-so-sunny disposition, and steer clear of the cowboy. Not Heather. She'd always admired his temperament, not to mention his strong stubborn jaw, deep-set brown eyes and equally dark slashing brows. Royce McKinnon was downright handsome in a rugged, manly-man sort of way.

His sober gaze fastened on her bare tummy, where a dainty silver butterfly ring pierced her navel. His stare, moving and mysterious, turned the simple act of breathing into a strenuous exercise. Her eyelids fluttered closed as she struggled for control. Three years ago this man had rocked her world. If her skittering nervousness at the moment was any indication, she hadn't succeeded in putting the past—rather, this man—behind her.

With one last gulp of air, she shoved her T-shirt back in place and hopped to her feet. Desperate for a moment to corral her frazzled nerves, she brushed at an imaginary wrinkle in her jeans, then fixed her lopsided ponytail.

At six feet two inches—minus the cowboy hat—the mayor of Nowhere, Texas, didn't exactly blend in with the gaggle of preschoolers running loose in the room. "If I'd known you were stopping in town I would have asked for time off." *Well, that was brilliant. He'll think I've been pining for him all these years.*

He cocked an eyebrow. "Some things never change."

"What's that supposed to mean?"

"I left a message on your cell phone."

The brooding, arrogant egghead was accusing *her* of not checking phone messages? Rolling her eyes, she sighed. "I see you brought along that trusty soapbox of yours."

"When you decide to grow up, I'll leave it at home."

The fact that he thought her plenty grown-up three years ago, when he'd kissed her, hung in the air between them like wet laundry on a windless day. "For your information, this isn't a job. Working at the day care is part of my student-teaching requirements."

Heather waited for a comeback that didn't come.

Royce's attention switched to the back of the room. Puzzled by the expression of deep sadness that filled his eyes as he watched the group of towheads devour their snacks, she touched his shirtsleeve.

The feel of the soft cotton material brought back a long-ago memory of Royce finding her bawling her head off behind the feed store. Even though her crying had embarrassed him, he'd offered her his shirtsleeve to wipe her nose. From that moment on Royce had been her hero.

After a while the novelty of his attention had worn off and she'd focused her efforts on ignoring his meddling presence. But nothing she'd done or said had made Royce go away and leave her alone—thank goodness. Because she would have been truly lost without this overbearing interfering man. For that reason alone she reined in her temper. "Look, if you're here to lecture me on failing to graduate next week with the rest of my class—"

"You're not graduating?"

Oh, crud. He didn't know? "Isn't that pretty obvious, since I didn't send you a graduation announcement?"

He rubbed the sexy little bump in the middle of his nose with his index finger. "I assumed I wasn't invited."

Did he think so little of her? Just because they'd shared one magical afternoon of intimacy and then…then…nothing didn't mean she hated him or didn't want him to celebrate her graduation. With all she'd put the man through over the years, he at least deserved to see her accept her degree. "I'm six credits short." His silence compelled her to explain. "I've signed up for the first and second summer sessions. If everything goes as planned I'll have my degree by summer's end."

"Degree in what now?"

"Psychology."

His brow dipped below the hat's brim. "Come again?"

"Psychology, with an emphasis on family and children."

His tanned complexion faded several shades, as if her choice of major and area of focus stunned him.

Perturbed by his reaction, she demanded, "What? You don't believe I would be good with kids?"

"You're nothing but a big kid yourself, Heather."

"People change. Maybe I wasn't the quintessential good-girl back in Nowhere, but I hope my past experiences will help other troubled children." She motioned to the crowded snack table. "Besides, I love kids."

A rude snort popped out of his mouth. He removed his hat, then tapped the edge against his thigh.

Shocked, she stared at the long, jagged scratch marring the underside of the brim. Another memory flashed through her mind: Royce parked outside the diner on Route 8, twenty miles outside of Nowhere, just over the Arkansas border. He'd sat in his truck for two hours, watching her and then boyfriend Buddy Mansfield through the plate-glass window. Then he'd followed them back to her trailer, his truck's brights beaming into the backs of their heads.

"You kept the hat," she whispered around the lump clogging her throat.

As if noticing the imperfection for the first time, he smoothed his thumb over the mark.

"I ruined the Stetson." *Because you ruined my plans to elope with Buddy.* Thank goodness Royce had. A marriage to the hometown bad-boy would have ended in disaster. Last she heard, Buddy was doing time in the Huntsville prison for armed robbery.

The lines around his Royce's eyes crinkled. "Only a fool would toss away a perfectly good hat because of a minor scratch."

An ache filled her chest. "Minor? I slashed the thing with a pocketknife." She hadn't known if she or Royce had been more stunned by the vengeful act.

"Yeah, you were full of piss and vinegar that evening."

She'd been thankful the moonless night had concealed the tears in her eyes as she'd struggled to find the words to apologize. Words she'd never found the courage to speak. Half of her had hoped she'd finally succeeded in driving Royce away. The other half had prayed he wouldn't give up on her.

When he shoved his fingers through a tuft of thick, reddish brown hair, the fluorescent lights in the ceiling highlighted a splash of silver along his temples.

"You've got gray hair," she blurted.

The corners of his mouth lifted in amusement. "Your name is on every one of them."

Her name and those of the rest of the good folks in Nowhere. Apparently, being rancher, mayor and saver of lost souls was taking a toll on the thirty-two-year-old.

The longer she studied him, the more she saw beyond his don't-mess-with-me expression. The rumpled state of his clothes reflected the long drive to the university. The tight lines around his mouth hinted at fatigue, not anger. She suspected a headache, not frustration, created the furrow in the middle of his brow. And exasperation didn't deepen the brown of his eyes—the dusky rings beneath them did.

Forbidding and unapproachable—not today. Exhausted and troubled—yes. But how could that be? Royce McKinnon had always been unshakable.

He checked his watch. "Can we talk in private?"

"I get off in fifteen minutes."

"I'll wait outside." He headed for the front door.

An uneasy feeling skittered down her spine as she watched his retreating back. Shoving the sensation aside, she hurried to the snack table to help Mrs. Richards quickly clean up the mess.

A short time later she sat in the front seat of Royce's big Dodge truck as he drove through the small campus side streets toward the rental house she shared with two roommates.

Royce hadn't said a word since he'd pulled out of the day-care parking lot. His silence bothered her more than the country music blasting from the CD player. He'd never been a talkative man…unless he was firing off one of his lectures on taking responsibility for one's own actions and other such drivel. She'd never given much consideration to his quiet nature, but right now she'd kill to know what was going on in that brooding mind of his.

Closing her eyes, she inhaled deeply. The clean crisp scent of his cologne wrapped around her like a warm hug, bringing with it a flash from the past: his mouth hovering over hers as they struggled to catch their breath.

Royce turned the corner and drove south on Conner Avenue, where most of the homes on the street were university rentals. She pointed out the windshield. "The bright yellow one." He parked at the curb in front of the house.

"What are those guys doing on your property?" he asked, referring to the two males sitting in rocking chairs, drinking beer on the porch.

"'Those guys' are my roommates."

"Roommates?"

His jaw worked as if he'd gotten a six-inch piece of rawhide caught between his teeth.

She hustled out of the truck and shut the door, cutting Royce off in mid sputter. Taking a deep breath, she marched up the sidewalk, determined to act like an adult even if he couldn't. A chorus of "Hey, Heather" greeted her as she climbed the porch steps. Ignoring Royce's hot breath fanning the back of her neck, she handled the introductions. "Seth, Joe, meet Royce McKinnon. He's the mayor of Nowhere, Texas."

"Cool," the two grunted in unison. Neither student stood or offered a hand in greeting. No one had ever accused Heather's roommates of having too much on the ball.

"Follow me," she muttered, moving across the porch. Once inside, she veered right, through a pair of French doors. "It's a two-bedroom house, but I converted the front parlor into a third bedroom." She set her purse on the chair in the corner.

Royce stopped in the doorway and glanced around. He

cleared his throat. "Do you mind?" Without waiting for an answer, he stepped farther into the room and shut the door.

She held her breath as his hand hovered over the door-knob. She didn't know whether to be disappointed or relieved when his large masculine fingers fell away without securing the lock.

Shoving his fists into the front pockets of his jeans, he rocked back on his heels. The stubborn lug looked so out of place standing in the peach-colored room with flower-stenciled walls and a mint-green velvet canopy hanging over her bed. Barbed wire was definitely more his style.

"Your room's nice, Heather."

A compliment? Admiring comments from Royce had been few and far between over the years. "Anything is better than that hovel I grew up in."

"If I'd known you cared, I'd have given you money to spruce up the trailer."

A knot formed in her chest. She *had* cared. Once, she'd started to paint the kitchen a soft buttercup yellow, but her old man, in one of his drunken rages, had stumbled and fallen against the wall, smearing the paint and cursing her for ruining his clothes. After enough of those "instances," she had realized caring was a waste of time and energy. Besides, acting as though living in a trash dump hadn't mattered to her gave Royce one less thing to butt his nose into.

She sat on the end of her bed, smoothed a hand over the white lace spread and swallowed twice before she could trust her voice.

"Have a seat," she said, motioning to the chair at the desk by the window.

As he crossed the room, she noticed the way his western shirt pulled at his shoulders. Noticed his backside, too.

The cowboy was in a category all his own. Ranching was physical work, but most of the ranchers she'd known growing up didn't have bodies like Royce. She'd touched a few of his impressive muscles when they'd kissed long ago, and this cowboy was in a category all his own. She wondered how he managed to stay in such great shape. She knew for a fact there wasn't a health club within fifty miles of Nowhere.

Some fool named Sapple had opened a small sawmill in the 1920s south of town, but like so many other East Texas sawmills, the place closed up five years later. Sapple and most of the loggers and their families had moved on, but a few people stayed behind. The town was officially named Nowhere when the interstate went in twenty-five miles away, leaving the local residents out in the middle of...nowhere. Aside from a barbershop, a bank, her father's feed store and a couple of mom-and-pop businesses, the town, surrounded by miles of ranchland and pine forests, boasted little else. If a person wanted excitement they had to get back on the interstate to find a popular restaurant or a honky-tonk.

Royce sat on her desk chair, expelled a long breath, then clasped his hands between his knees and stared at the floor.

Stomach clenching with apprehension, she asked, "What's so important you couldn't have told me over the phone?"

Her question brought his head up, and she stopped breathing at the solemn expression in his dark eyes. "What I have to say should be said in person."

She almost blurted, *Three years ago you had no trouble telling me that our kiss had been a terrible mistake. That you didn't want to see me again. That you didn't want me to come back to Nowhere.* Instead, she settled for "A long time ago you had no trouble telling me over the phone to get lost."

He stiffened, then cleared his throat and studied the *Titanic* movie poster hanging on the wall beside her bed. He turned his attention to her face, embarrassment and regret pinching his features. This time she looked away.

"How are you situated for money?"

The news must really be bad if Royce was stalling. "If I get the job that I applied for at the law library, I'll be able to make ends meet this summer." She'd already exhausted all the partial scholarships and government grants she'd been eligible for during the first four years of school. From then on, she'd had to work to pay for tuition and books, expenses and rent. She hated admitting it, hated that she was still dependent on him, but without Royce's more-than-generous Christmas and birthday checks she would have had to drop out of college long ago.

Shifting on the chair, he removed his checkbook from the back pocket of his jeans. She had only one pen on her desk, a neon-pink one with a bright yellow feather and beaded ribbon attached to the end. She pressed her lips together to keep from smiling at the disgusted expression on his face when he tried to see around the feather as he wrote out the check.

"I don't want your money, Royce." Her face heated at the lie, but she felt compelled to offer a token protest.

He didn't hand the check to her. Instead, he set the draft on top of her psychology text. "For someone who had to be forced to go to college, you've hung in there and beaten the odds."

Two compliments in one day. This must be some sort of record for Royce. But knowing that she'd done something he approved of made her feel good. Proud. Vulnerable. She smiled sheepishly. "To be honest, I'm a little surprised I didn't drop out my first year."

"Just think. If you hadn't been involved with that group of misfits who held up the Quick Stop, you might never have gone to college."

Heather groaned. "Please. Let's not bring that up." She'd just as soon forget that fateful July night seven years ago when Royce had bailed her out of the county jail after being arrested in connection with the gas station holdup. She'd been using the restroom, unaware that the other teens had planned to rob the place. Because she hadn't been in the store during the robbery, Royce had been able to convince the judge to let her off the hook. But the judge had added a condition of her own—college.

"The expression on your face when the judge announced your sentence was priceless. One would have thought you'd been sentenced to death, not college," Royce chuckled, then his face sobered.

"What are your plans after you get your degree in August?"

"I want to work with children. Socioeconomically disadvantaged kids."

He started to protest, but she held up a hand. "You're thinking I wouldn't be a good role model, right?" Why was it so hard for Royce to believe she'd changed since going away to school?

Shrugging, he slouched in the chair. "As long as I've known you, you've always been the one receiving help, not giving it."

Ouch. That stung. Irritated with herself for allowing his comment to hurt, she changed the subject. "Enough reminiscing. Why the surprise visit?"

"I wish there were an easier way to say this." He dragged a hand down his face.

The suspense rattled her nerves. "Spit it out, Royce."

"Your father's dead."

She opened her mouth to suck in air, but nothing happened. Her lungs froze as her body processed the shock. After several seconds, her chest thawed, and she gulped a lungful of oxygen.

"I'm sorry, Heather." He leaned forward again and squeezed her hand.

Numbly, she stared at the tanned hand, wondering whether the rough, calloused touch of his skin against hers or the news of her father's death shook her more.

"How—?" Her eyes watered, surprising her. After all these years, she didn't think she had any emotion left for her father. That she still felt *something* for the old man made her stomach queasy.

"A fire."

Her gaze flew to his face. "The feed store burned down?"

He tugged his hand loose, and she bit her lip to keep from protesting the loss of his warmth and gentleness.

"The trailer caught fire. The county fire investigator believes it was accidental."

No need to explain the gory details. As a child, how many times had she gone to bed, only to get up in the middle of the night to use the bathroom and find her father asleep on the couch, a lit cigarette dangling from between his fingers?

"A tourist passing by called 911. By the time the volunteer fire department got there..." Royce shook his head, sympathy in his eyes. "Nothing but a burned-out shell remained."

"When?"

"Late yesterday afternoon."

Her father was dead. She was alone in the world. Really *alone.* But maybe that was okay. Even when her father was alive she'd been alone. Still, Royce had always been there.

And he's here now.

Royce stood. "I'll wait in the truck while you pack."

Dazed, she mumbled, "Pack?"

His eyebrows dipped. "For the funeral."

"Funeral?" Why wasn't anything making sense? She rubbed her temples, wincing at the onset of a headache.

He lowered his voice. "There's usually a funeral after someone dies, Heather."

"Why bother? No one will show up." Not one person in Nowhere had liked her father, including her. The man had been an alcoholic, chain-smoking, card-gambling jerk.

"People will want to pay their respects to you." He moved toward the door. "We'll keep the service simple."

"Simple." She laughed at the absurdity of the whole situation. "I guess good ol' Dad handled the cremation himself."

Royce's eyebrows shot straight up into his hairline. "I realize you didn't have the best relationship with the man. But there are times when you have to do what's right. This is one of them."

Wondering if he could see the steam rising from the top of her head, she popped off the bed. "Ever since my mother ran off, you've pestered, nagged and lectured me! Well, I've had enough. Find yourself another hopeless cause to champion."

His head snapped back as if she'd slapped him, then a shuttered look crept into his eyes. "Pack your bags, Heather." His tone could have freeze-dried a whole cow. "You're coming home."

Home? She'd never considered the filthy, rattrap trailer she'd grown up in a home. Now, thanks to her father, there wasn't even that.

And why would the good folks of Nowhere want to pay their respects to a girl who'd done nothing but cause them grief during her rebellious adolescent years? She wouldn't last ten minutes in town before they ran her out. "No funeral. I'm not going back with you."

Mr. Responsibility pinched the bridge of his nose, and guilt stabbed her. Undoubtedly, he'd already put in a hard day of ranching, then stuck his mayor cap on and solved the town's problems, after which he'd driven three hundred miles to College Station. She didn't doubt he'd return to the ranch tonight, wake up at dawn and start the whole boring process all over again.

"I'll make the funeral arrangements. All you have to do is show up."

She shook her head, hating the way her throat swelled and tears burned her eyes. *Darn!* She would not cry for her father. He didn't deserve one single tear from her.

Royce's brown eyes turned stormy. "You might consider yourself a grown-up, but when are you going to start acting like one?"

Ashamed to shove the burden of her father's burial on Royce, she forced the words past her lips. "I'm not going back."

The muscle along his jaw ticked. "What about the feed store?"

As far as she cared, the building could sit and rot before she'd ever set foot inside it again. "I don't want the business. Sell it."

"You don't have to decide right this minute."

"No, really. Just get rid of the place." She lifted her chin, determined to stand her ground.

"Think about it some more. In the meantime, I'll contact a Realtor."

When he headed for the door, her heart skipped a beat. Part of her wanted him to leave so she could sort through the mishmash of emotions knotting her insides, yet part of her yearned for the comfort of his physical presence. *Darn!* She'd handled his visit badly. But for the life of her she didn't know how to make things right.

"Royce."

He stopped but kept his back to her.

"Thank you. For coming all this way."

A quick nod, and then he was gone.

Just gone. She should be happy she'd escaped without having to suffer through one of his infamous hour-long sermons. Why then did she wish he'd stayed and lectured her?

Because you still haven't gotten over him!

She flung herself across the bed and buried her face in the pillows, fighting the sting of more tears. Deep in her heart she believed she'd made the right decision not to go back with Royce. Summer classes started soon. And any day now she'd hear about the job at the law library.

Then an image of Royce's tired face behind the steering wheel of his truck flashed through her mind. She rolled off the bed, went to her desk and lifted the check he'd left there. *A thousand dollars!* Her eyes zeroed in on the memo line in the bottom left-hand corner…*Happy 25th birthday, Heather.*

He hadn't forgotten that tomorrow was her birthday.

She threw herself back on the bed and burst into tears.

Chapter Two

Oh, hell.

Royce hefted the last hay bale into his truck bed, then stopped to watch the cloud of dust trailing the Ford pickup that barreled toward the barn. After checking on the cattle this morning, he'd called the fire inspector and received permission to have the damaged trailer hauled to the dump. The inspector had officially closed the case, declaring Melvin Henderson's death accidental. Royce had hoped he'd get out of here before his nosy foreman returned from an overnight visit with his ailing sister. No such luck.

Guilt nagged him at the uncharitable thought. Luke was like family. The foreman had hired on at the ranch ten years ago when Royce's uncle had been diagnosed with cancer and been given only a few months to live. At the time Luke was fifty-five. Royce's uncle had died in August, and the following winter his aunt had succumbed to pneumonia. After Royce had buried his aunt, he'd insisted Luke move out of the small room at the back of the barn and into the main house.

The truck came to a stop next to the corral. As soon as Luke opened the door, his old hound dog, Bandit, hopped down from the front seat. Tail wagging, the animal hurried toward Royce as fast as his arthritic legs would carry him.

Royce scratched Bandit's ear. "How's Martha feeling?"

"Spry as a spring chick." Luke grumbled a four-letter word. "There wasn't nothin' wrong with the woman in the first place. Just lonely is all. No wonder she ain't never married all these years. Can't keep her trap shut for nothin'. Yakkin' about this, yakkin' about that. I had to get out of there before my ears shriveled up and fell off my head."

Luke and Martha were twins, and Martha took great pleasure in bossing her brother around. Royce swallowed a laugh at the disgruntled expression on his foreman's face, then suggested, "Why don't you invite her to stay at the ranch for the summer. We've got plenty of room."

"Hell, no! You think I want that old biddy askin' me if I got fresh drawers on every mornin'?" Luke pulled a pouch of Skoal from the front pocket of his overalls. "How'd Heather take the news?"

"Better than I'd hoped." He hadn't expected her to feel much of anything at learning of her father's death. Then he'd caught the glimmer of tears in her baby blues. The lost expression on her face had convinced him that she'd been deeply affected. He supposed no matter what kind of relationship Heather and her father had had over the years, a part of her had always yearned for his love.

"She comin' home after graduatin'?"

"She won't be graduating next week." Royce slammed the tailgate shut and wiped his sweaty palms down the front of his threadbare jeans. He wasn't in the mood to discuss Heather Henderson with anybody—not even Luke.

Last night had been hell. He'd returned from College Station right around midnight and had fallen into bed exhausted and agitated. He'd lain awake for hours, tossing and turning, his insides and outsides tied in knots.

After his accident three years ago, he'd have sworn he had put Heather behind him. Heck, he'd even had a couple of affairs. A summer fling with a tourist and an off-and-on thing with a local divorcée, whom he'd probably still be seeing if she hadn't taken a job in Arizona.

But one glimpse at Heather—just one glimpse—and all the feelings for her that he'd thought long dead and buried had rushed to the surface, stunning him with their intensity.

After shoving a wad of chewing tobacco in his mouth, Luke offered Bandit a small pinch and the dog ran off and buried it beneath the sugar maple tree by the front porch. "How come she ain't gettin' her degree?"

"She still has a couple of classes to finish, first."

"After that, is she comin' home?"

"Nope." Not if he had his way. Royce marched toward the barn and the old fart followed him like a pesky fly.

"Full of 'nopes' lately, ain't you."

"Yep."

Luke stopped inside the barn doors. "You ain't said how she was?"

"She's fine." Royce searched through the junk in the corner for a bushel basket. *Fine* didn't come close to describing Heather. She was more than fine. She was beautiful, full of energy and life, and she possessed a new self-confidence that hadn't been there the last time he'd seen her.

"Just fine, huh?"

"Yep." He knew he was being an ass. But he couldn't seem to find the words to tell Luke about Heather's desire to work with children. About how *right* she'd looked sprawled on the floor buried under a pile of preschoolers. He couldn't tell Luke that it had almost physically hurt to watch her wrestle with the kids.

Luke had been the one to find Royce lying unconscious alongside the road. Royce had awakened from surgery and the doctor had given him the bad news. In his own way, Luke had grieved along with Royce. And when the time had come to stop grieving and move on, Luke had been the one to plant his boot heel in Royce's backside and force him out of his depression, and back into the world of the living.

Compelled to say more, Royce added, "Heather seemed excited about getting her degree at the end of the summer."

"What kind of degree?"

"In counseling, psychology to be exact. She plans to work with disadvantaged kids."

Bandit barked somewhere outside the barn and Luke hollered at him to hush. "What about the funeral?"

"There isn't going to be a funeral."

"Why not?"

"Heather doesn't want one."

"Can't blame the poor gal."

"I spoke with Pastor Gates, and he's agreed to say a few words about Henderson during the service on Sunday."

"Don't deserve much more."

No argument there. Melvin Henderson had been a first-class loser. He hadn't had a nice word for anyone the whole time he'd been alive.

A stream of tobacco juice sailed past Royce's face.

"How long ago did that gal start college?" asked Luke.

"Seven years."

The geezer made a whistling sound as he sucked in air

through the gap between his front teeth. "Least she didn't up and quit on you."

Pride surged through Royce. When Heather had chosen college over juvenile detention, he'd never expected her to last more than a semester or two. "You're right. She might have taken her sweet time, but she didn't quit." He shoved aside several wooden crates, until he found a dented basket; then he carried it to the other side of the barn, where the freshly picked garden vegetables were stored.

Switching the ball of chew to his other cheek, Luke motioned to the loaded pickup. "I thought you was ridin' fence today."

"Change of plans. I'm meeting with a Realtor to put the feed store on the market."

"Ain't that Heather's business?"

Should be. Heather might have done some growing up since going away to college, but she still ran the opposite direction when faced with the big *R*—responsibility. "She doesn't want anything to do with the store."

"Don't seem right."

Where Heather was concerned, nothing was ever as it *seemed.* If Royce were honest with himself—something he tried to avoid at all costs in order to keep his sanity—he'd admit Heather had left a void in his life when she'd gone off to college. Prior to that, his weeks had been filled with chasing after her, righting her wrongs, fixing her mistakes. When she'd graduated high school and moved to College Station his life had become…well, dull.

"It's her decision, Luke."

"Since when did you ever give that gal a say-so?"

"She's had plenty of say-so's." Like the damn fool major she'd ended up in. *Psychology.* How the heck a person who'd made a mess of her own life thought she could help straighten out someone else's baffled him.

"So you're tyin' up all the loose ends for her?"

"Haven't I always kept her life tight and tidy?" Royce rubbed a hand down his face, regretting the testy remark. Heather hadn't asked for his help; he'd offered. Now, if he could only figure out why he was so all-fired pissed off about it.

"You think she's gonna look for a job 'round here after graduatin'?"

God, he hoped not. For the sake of his heart he prayed Heather would find a job far, far away from Nowhere. "She didn't say."

"What about the car?"

He glanced at the yellow Mustang sitting under a tarp at the back of the barn. His chest tightened when he thought of how he'd helped her purchase the vehicle after she'd worked her tail off to pay for the thing. He hadn't even had to convince her to leave the Mustang behind when she left for college. She'd known the car was safer in the barn than on campus.

"Luke, I don't have time to worry about Heather and her plans. I've got enough troubles with the town's sewer system deteriorating as we speak."

"Heard anything from the governor?"

"His aide called." Royce carried the bushel of vegetables out of the barn, opened the tailgate and set them in the truck bed next to the hay bales. He pulled a bandana from his back pocket and mopped his brow. At ten in the morning, the temperature hovered near eighty degrees. The above-normal temperature for late May promised a long, hot Texas summer. "To a certain extent the governor is sympathetic."

"Sympathetic how?"

"If Nowhere turns in a sizable campaign donation, the governor may be able to pull some strings and move us up on the list for government funding for a new sewer."

"Aw, let him blow it out his ear. There ain't enough money in this town to build a meetin' hall, let alone throw away on a politician who don't give a rat's turd about our little map dot."

"Amen. I refuse to use our five hundred and fifteen citizens' tax dollars to finance the governor's reelection campaign, when I can't stand the guy in the first place." Royce shut the tailgate.

His face puckering like a withered apple, Luke asked, "What'll you do 'bout the sewer?"

Royce wished that every business in town had its own septic system. But during the 1940s the federal government had laid down sewer pipe as part of a work program to improve the quality of life in rural areas. As far as Royce was concerned, his town's quality of life was disappearing faster than the water flushed down the toilets. "With a little luck, the system should hold out another year."

He hopped into the truck, then shut the door before his foreman decided to ride along. "By next spring, I'll figure out something." And he would. He'd never before let down the citizens of Nowhere. One way or another he'd find the money to at least repair the sewer. He turned the key and gunned the motor. "Don't expect me back anytime soon. After I meet with the Realtor, I plan to drop off the hay and vegetables at the Wilkinsons' place."

Another brown glob of tobacco flew past the truck window and landed with a *splat* near the front tire. "When you gonna stop givin' everybody handouts?"

"I'm the mayor, Luke. I won't stand by and watch four kids starve because their father's out of work with a broken back and their mother's run off to God-knows-where with who-knows-whom." Right then, Heather's mother came to mind, making Royce wonder what it was about Nowhere that had women running off in the middle of the night.

"Broken back, my ass."

Royce would have to call Martha later and thank her for twisting her brother's undershorts in a knot this morning. "Kenny will be over next week to help with chores." Kenny, the eldest Wilkinson boy, helped Luke around the ranch in exchange for hay for his rodeo horse.

"Just what I need. A snot-nosed brat followin' me 'round." Luke called for Bandit, then shuffled toward the house.

Grinning, Royce drove off. His foreman did a lot of complaining about the smart-mouthed teen, but Luke appreciated the kid's company. It was a win-win situation. The boy was good company for Luke, and Luke was good company for Kenny, who needed a swift kick in the butt from time to time—something Luke had perfected on Royce over the years.

At the end of the ranch drive, Royce took the county road south. Tall pines bordered the asphalt, some as high as one hundred and twenty feet. Most of the trees were second-generation. The area had been gutted by the lumber industry at the turn of the twentieth century. The once-dense pine forests were now broken up with large sections of ranch land. Sprinkled in among the yellow pines were clusters of southern red oak, sweetgum and water oak. This part of East Texas received enough rainfall to be classified as an upper wetland area, which meant that spring put on a pretty impressive display. His favorite tree was the flowering dogwood, with its abundant white blooms.

The area boasted a great fishing lake. During the summer months, campers took advantage of the wilderness that surrounded Nowhere and Lake Wright several miles to the northeast. The town's small business owners relied heavily on summer tourism to keep afloat. That was one of Royce's goals as mayor—to find a way to bring more tourists to the area.

Pressing the gas pedal until the speedometer hovered near seventy, he switched his thoughts to the feed store. Over the years, the local ranchers had begun purchasing the bulk of their supplies from big discount chains along the interstate. But in emergencies, or to save time, they shopped at Henderson Feed for smaller items. For the past two days the business had remained closed. Royce needed to find someone to work in the store until the building sold.

Fifteen minutes later, he swung the truck into a parking spot outside the dilapidated redbrick building. Frank Telmon waited by the door, briefcase in hand, jowls sagging two inches lower than usual. The Realtor must have bad news.

"Frank." Royce greeted him as he climbed the steps and unlocked the door with the key he'd confiscated from the store register yesterday. He'd had to enter the stockroom through a broken window to get inside. He'd ransacked the place, searching for bookkeeping records or any paperwork that would show what kind of financial shape the business was in. All he'd found were old tax documents, a few bank statements and the store ledger with the names and numbers of suppliers and bookies. He'd handed the ledger over to Telmon before heading down to the university.

Telmon, who doubled as an accountant, followed Royce inside. "I'm afraid I have unpleasant news."

"Figured as much." Royce walked to the back of the store, then leaned against the checkout counter next to the outdated cash register.

"Henderson wasn't much of a businessman." Frank set his briefcase on the counter. "I went over the papers you dropped off at the office." He removed a file folder from inside.

"And..."

Shaking his head, Frank pursed his lips so hard the corners of his mouth disappeared into his cheeks. "I don't understand how he stayed in business as long as he did."

"Give me the bare facts." Royce should have figured selling the store wouldn't be as easy as he'd hoped.

"The business is two years in arrears on taxes. The building needs a major overhaul, and inventory is basically nonexistent. Nothing short of a miracle and a hell of a lot of cash will put this business back in the black."

Great. Just great. He'd hoped there would be enough money left over from the sale of the store for Heather to live on until she found a job and an apartment after graduation. "What do you suggest putting the place on the market for?"

A harsh bark fired from Telmon's mouth, the sound smacking off the rotting brick walls like a rifle shot. "Sell? You won't be able to *give* the place away."

As Royce glanced around, he was hard put to disagree. Swirls of yellowish brown water stains covered the ceiling—a leaky roof. A musty, damp smell saturated the air inside the building—mold. The plank floor groaned, creaked and popped—wood rot. The mortar in the brick walls had all but crumbled away, leaving holes big enough to shove a fist into. *Oh, hell.* The building needed a wrecking ball, not a For Sale sign. "Heather doesn't want anything to do with the feed store. The place will have to go on the market as is."

Nodding, Telmon returned the file to his briefcase. "First smart decision the girl's made in a long time."

Royce bristled at the insult to Heather. *He* himself could talk about her that way, but he sure didn't approve of others criticizing her. Heather was smarter than most people realized. Although she'd skipped a lot of classes and had driven her teachers nuts with her rebellious behavior, she'd scored higher on her college entrance exams—Scholastic Aptitude Test—than two-thirds of her high school graduating class.

The Realtor shut his briefcase. "If you're sure she has no plans to make repairs before listing the place, then I'll write up a contract and get back to you in a couple of days."

Royce offered his hand. "Thanks for your help."

"My pleasure." Walking toward the front door, Telmon shook his head, his loose jowls reminding Royce of a bulldog.

As soon as the door closed behind the man, Royce flipped open his cell phone. He'd give Heather the bare facts, then let Telmon answer any questions she had. His finger froze over the keypad.

Once Heather graduated and sold the store, she'd no longer be his concern. And maybe, just maybe he'd finally be able to put the memories of their passionate kisses behind him for good. He waited to feel a sense of relief—it didn't come. Annoyed, he smacked the counter with an open palm.

No, his sanity wouldn't stand a chance if Heather decided to move back home. He should thank his lucky stars she wanted nothing to do with Nowhere.

Or him.

Chapter Three

"Drat!" Heather sputtered into the warm shower spray, as she listened to her cell phone in the bedroom play the theme song from *Gilligan's Island.* Lathering her hair, she sang along to the music. Already thirty minutes late to a pregraduation party for two of her friends, she didn't have time to chat. Since she'd be starting her new job at the law library tomorrow, she wouldn't be able to watch her friends graduate at the Saturday-morning ceremony. Tonight's party would be her last chance to say goodbye and wish her friends well.

Abruptly, Gilligan shut up.

A moment later, the phone went off again. *Okay, already!* Worried that her supervisor might be calling with a change in Heather's work schedule, she ignored the shampoo in her hair and turned off the water. She grabbed the towel from the hook on the door and made a mad dash into the bedroom. "Hello?"

"It's me."

The sound of Royce McKinnon's low, rusty voice shot a bolt of heat through Heather's body, causing the phone to slip from her slick hands, smack the desk, then land on the floor with a *thunk.* The towel followed. Naked, shampoo bubbles streaming down her back and front, she gaped at the phone, which lay next to her big toe.

As if in a trance, she lifted her gaze to the mirror on the wall in front of her, and gasped at the bright red color rolling like great ocean waves down her body. She looked as if she'd been dunked in a life-size jar of maraschino-cherry juice. The garbled sound of a human voice pulled her out of her stupor. *Good grief!* He couldn't *see* her naked body. She scooped the phone off the floor. "Hello?"

"Is everything all right, Heather?"

"Yes. Just a minute." Annoyed by her adolescent reaction, she set the cell on her desk, then swiped the beach-size towel off the floor and wrapped the terry cloth around herself. Twice.

She drew in a deep, calming breath and put the phone up to her ear. "Sorry. I'm here."

"Did I call at a bad time?"

More than likely, he assumed he'd interrupted an in-between-class quickie with one of the porch boys—her roommates. "You caught me in the shower."

Dead silence. Then he cleared his throat. "I'll call later."

"No, no. I'm covered now." She swallowed a groan at the stupid remark. Time to turn the conversation in a different direction. "The funeral…did everything get—"

"I took care of things."

Although she assumed he would follow through on his promise to arrange her father's burial, she'd been hoping for at least a brief phone call explaining the details. Evidently, he hadn't thought she deserved even that. Not that she could blame him, after she'd shoved the responsibility onto his shoulders. "Thank you for handling the arrangements." She tensed, waiting for some kind of smart remark about accountability, commitment...whatever. Only a faint huff filtered through the connection. Odd, she could have sworn the huff sounded tired.

Like a swift kick in the butt, guilt caught her by surprise. Of course Royce was worn-out. He arranged not only her father's funeral, but more than likely he handled everything else that had come up as a result of the trailer fire. He had every reason to be short with her—

"I'm calling about the store," he said.

A twinge of disappointment pinched her. Stupidly, she'd hoped he'd contacted her because he wanted to find out how *she'd* been coping with her father's death. Agitated, she shoved a hand into her soapy hair, then glared at the sticky residue coating her fingers. "What about the store?"

"An offer came in."

"There's a buyer already?"

"Yeah. Surprised the heck out of me, too. The owner of a chain of ranch-supply stores in eastern Arkansas called F & F Supply is interested in buying the business. He doesn't seem concerned about the condition of the building and money isn't an object."

"If he's rich, why doesn't he build a new store?"

"Telmon thinks he's looking for a tax write-off. The guy checks out. He's legit."

"But—"

"The good news is that after the sale, there'll be money left to tide you over until you figure out what you're going to do after graduation."

She struggled to summon some excitement. "Great."

"You don't sound 'great.' What's the matter?" he demanded.

"I'm just surprised that anyone would want to buy the

business." What was wrong with her? The store was her last remaining tie to Nowhere—except for Royce. She should be elated someone wanted the dump. If she sold the business, she'd have no reason to return there. All the better. Nothing waited for her in Nowhere anymore.

Crazy as it seemed, the thought of saying a final goodbye to her birthplace saddened her. After her mother had abandoned her, she'd stopped thinking of Nowhere as her home…it had been just a place she'd survived.

"The offer is one hundred and fifty thousand."

"That's all?"

"Considering the financial mess your father made of the business, the amount is damn generous. You'll be left with five thousand after paying the bank note, back taxes and creditors."

"Oh." Sighing, she collapsed on the end of the bed.

"Heather—"

The ominous undertone in his voice set off a warning bell in her head.

"You're not having second thoughts, are you?"

"Maybe." If not for Royce's visit last week she'd probably have jumped at the offer.

But Royce *had* shown up at the day care and he'd sent her world spinning. Since then, not an hour had gone by that she hadn't reminisced about the past. About the one time they'd kissed that Saturday afternoon in April three years ago…about the night she'd called him a month later before her end-of-the-year finals in May to accept his offer to spend the summer at his ranch…about the cruel way he'd rejected her, insisting that their kiss had been a big mistake.

If not for his unexpected visit last week, Heather would

never have believed that Royce might have been lying three years ago when he'd told her to get lost. But she'd caught the naked longing in his eyes when their gazes first clashed—the same longing she'd seen when they'd kissed that first time. Heather was convinced Royce felt…something for her. Why he denied his feelings was a mystery she was determined to solve.

Her father's death had brought Royce back into her life. This time she wasn't letting him push her away until she understood why he'd rejected her. The fact that Royce wanted her to stay away from Nowhere was her first clue that he was hiding something from her.

The store was the excuse she needed to return home and do a little digging into the past.

"Listen, you can't save the business unless you come up with a truckload of money."

"Sheesh, Royce. Have a little faith in me, will you?" Just like all the other good folks in Nowhere, Royce believed her nothing more than an airhead.

"You're not exactly the queen of capability and commitment."

"I've changed since going away to school."

"You haven't changed *that* much."

Royce had just laid down the gauntlet. "Oh?"

"You don't really want to run the store."

She cringed. Unloading sacks of corn feed held as much appeal as gutting fish on a hot, humid day. But pretending to care about the business was as good an excuse to go home as any. If she could persuade her professors to allow her to take her two remaining classes by correspondence, she'd still earn her degree by the end of the summer. Then if things didn't work out with Royce, she'd leave Nowhere, find a job and begin a new chapter in her life. "I could run the business until I get a better offer."

"A better offer? You're kidding." Yep. The hint of desperation in his voice convinced her that he was harboring a secret. "Heather…you are joking, aren't you?"

"I'm not ready to sell."

"The store isn't a game or a toy you can toss aside when you're tired of playing around."

"I never thought of the business as a toy."

"C'mon, Heather."

"Decline the offer." As soon as the words left her mouth, she wanted to call them back. Change her mind. Run for cover. There was no guarantee she'd even find the answers she sought, and if she did…could she handle the truth?

"Haven't I always looked out for your best interests?"

"Whether you approve or not, Royce, I'm coming home."

Returning to Nowhere might prove to be the most rash, absurd, worst decision she'd ever made in her life—so far. But once she gave voice to her plan, a sense of peace filled her.

"You're not dropping out of college. Christ, Heather. You're too close to getting a degree to quit now."

"What makes you think I won't get my degree?"

"Heather—"

"Listen up, buckaroo. I've managed to stay in college and not drop out. I've managed a B average in all my classes—and that's a lot of classes over seven years. I've managed to work several different part-time jobs to help support me while in school. I've managed—"

"Stop." His shout startled Heather into silence. "I didn't mean that the way it sounded," he added in a quieter voice. "But managing a business, an almost bankrupt business, is a lot of responsibility."

She admitted that he had every right to believe she'd run when the going got tough. She'd done plenty of running in the past. Well, actions spoke louder than words. She was through running.

Proving she could oversee the store would be the first step in earning his respect. And for some reason, she yearned for Royce's respect. "I appreciate your concern, but I've made up my mind."

A burst of pure, sweet rebellion broke free inside her, and she reveled in the exhilarating sensation. She unknotted the towel over her breasts and flung it across the room. Stark naked, chin high, she faced her adversary…through the cell phone signal. "It's time *I,* not *you,* decide what's best for me."

"Heather. Stay put."

"Goodbye, Royce."

"I'm warning you, Heather—"

She flipped the phone shut, cutting him off in mid threat. After returning to the bathroom, she finished her shower, then shimmied into a pair of sparkling purple panties and a matching bra. She tingled with excitement and fear. Dealing with the feed store on her own terms would help her put the past to rest and determine her future—with or without Royce.

Monday she'd visit her professors and explain about her father's death and her wish to settle his estate. She was positive they'd allow her to complete her courses by correspondence. Tomorrow, she'd quit her job at the law library and put an ad in the paper to sublet the house. If all went well, she'd return to Nowhere by the first week of June.

Now, if she could only figure out how to save her father's business. An idea started to form. If she used psychological profiles to chart the wants and needs of customers… Later tonight, after returning from the graduation party, she'd sit down and draw up a business plan.

"OH, MY! What is such a handsome devil doing in the middle of Nowhere?" The Marilyn Monroe look-alike's sultry voice drifted over Heather's bus seat, startling her like a slap to the back of the head.

Leaning forward, she peered around the gray-haired granny she'd shared the trip with from College Station to Nowhere. The little old lady continued to snore, oblivious to the Greyhound's turn into the almost-empty church lot.

Holy cow. Heather's thoughts echoed Marilyn Monroe's sentiments. She stared at the lone male leaning against a black Dodge four-by-four pickup. The vehicle was big and menacing and familiar.

So was the man.

Eight days had passed since she'd informed Royce of her plan to return to Nowhere and run the feed store. She hadn't expected to find him waiting for her bus in the middle of a Thursday afternoon. She'd intended to arrive in town without anyone the wiser. She swallowed back a sigh. Some things never changed—like "the mayor" knowing her every move…even before she did.

Tall, broad and dark, he resembled a bad-boy more than a rancher. He wore scuffed cowboy boots, a black T-shirt tucked into tight, faded button-fly jeans and the same battered Stetson, with the brim tilted low over his forehead to block the late-afternoon sun.

Good heavens, the man was a looker. The driver swung the bus in a wide arc until the front end faced the street. Her attention remained on the lone figure by the truck. His powerful physique lent him an air of authority. Not that he needed an air. He came by his demanding, bossy nature naturally.

When the bus stopped, she slipped her purse over her shoulder and grabbed her backpack from under the seat in front of her. She was the only fool getting off in Nowhere.

Marilyn Monroe smacked her gum. "Go get him, honey."

Heather's heart thumped. But it had nothing to do with the rancher's sex appeal and everything to do with his temper. With steady steps she made her way to the front of the bus, her fingernails sinking like talons into the cushioned seat backs.

You shouldn't have hung up on him.

A tiny voice in her head insisted it wasn't too late to turn back, reclaim her seat and ride to the next town, to forget proving anything to anyone. Royce would finally be able to wash his hands of her, and she'd never have to set foot in Nowhere again.

Stupidly, she ignored the voice.

No matter how afraid she was of the answer, she couldn't walk away from the chance to finally learn why Royce had ended their relationship before it had even had a chance to get off the ground.

And while she was unearthing the past, she might as well show the good folks of Nowhere that Heather Henderson had changed for the better. As she neared the door she cringed inwardly. *You're in for the fight of your life.*

When her shoes hit the pavement, a gust of hot wind smacked her in the face and blasted her loose hair six inches in the air. Her legs jiggled like cooked noodles, and she locked her knees, refusing to appear weak in front of her nemesis. She shielded her eyes from the sun's glare while the driver unloaded the two suitcases and two boxes of college mementos she'd brought home with her.

A bead of perspiration trickled between her breasts. Royce's relaxed pose didn't fool her. *He's ticked.* Obviously, she wouldn't be receiving a warm mayoral welcome and the key to the city.

The bus driver shut and locked the storage door. "Have a nice stay, ma'am."

She mumbled a quick thank-you. A second later, the motor coach shifted gear, belched a cloud of black exhaust and drove off leaving…

Her.

And him.

And the sweltering June heat.

He wore mirrored shades, but a sixth sense told her he looked her straight in the eye.

In one smooth motion, he removed the glasses. From fifteen feet away his hot brown glare threatened to melt her. If he were any closer, she'd burst into flames.

"Heather."

Oh, man. He was more than ticked. His lips hadn't moved when he spoke.

She lifted her chin. "Royce."

"I thought I told you to stay put."

The hairs on the back of her neck stood up and wiggled in indignation. "You should realize by now I don't listen too well."

He rubbed a hand across his brow, and Heather almost felt sorry for him.

"You're bound and determined to take the store on?"

"Yes."

"Until you get a better offer?"

Let him think that. If Royce were to find out why she was really in Nowhere, he'd hit the ground running. "Yes."

He studied her as if he wanted more than her words as reassurance. "Where are you staying?" He asked the question warily, as if he feared she intended to move into his ranch house.

"I'd planned to live in the store." Rent-free, no commute. Life couldn't get any better. And a little distance between her and Royce was a good thing—just until he got used to her being around again.

"You can't stay at the store. The place is a dump. Besides, where would you sleep?"

"There's a large closet off the storeroom. I can fit a cot in there."

"I saw the commode in the back, but what about bathing?"

Next thing, he'd be asking what she planned to do about toilet paper! "The storeroom has a showerhead." She just hoped the water ran clear and didn't come out all rusty and smelling like dead fish.

He fumed in silence, as if contemplating how to throw her over his shoulder and haul her back to College Station.

"Fine. We'll take your things over to the store, then head out to the ranch. There's an old bed in the attic you can have, and the mini fridge in the barn."

No more arguing? *Amazing.* "Thanks. And if it's all right with you, I'd like to get my car so I have a way to get around."

"Your father's truck wasn't destroyed in the fire. It's parked behind the store."

She helped Royce load her luggage and the boxes into the pickup bed, then hopped in on the passenger side. "I'll use the truck for business and the Mustang for pleasure." She flashed a smile across the seat.

Frowning, he turned the key and the motor roared to life. "You're sure about this?"

She crossed her fingers. "Absolutely."

"I hope to hell you know what you're doing, Heather."

So do I, Royce. So do I.

Chapter Four

Royce gripped the steering wheel until pains shot up his forearm. Five minutes on the road with Heather and he felt like kicking a fence post barefoot.

Without even trying, the woman lit his fuse. As if he'd stepped on a land mine, she scattered his emotions and shredded his common sense into useless fragments of illogic—and she'd accomplished all that without uttering a single word since getting in the truck!

While he'd waited for the bus to arrive, he'd had a long talk with himself. He'd decided that the only way to survive Heather this summer was to avoid her.

One way or another he had to resist the natural urge to run to her aid every time she got herself in a pickle. He figured it was only a matter of time before she hopped a bus back to College Station, or accepted another offer for the property.

While Heather was playing store, he had a whole list of things to keep him busy this summer. Aside from looking after his small herd of Angus cattle, he had plenty of ranch repairs that needed his attention and if he still had time on his hands, he'd paint the blasted house. Add the extra responsibilities of being a mayor and he doubted he'd run into Heather more than once or twice during the entire summer—if she lasted that long.

With a disgusted huff, he gave in to the urge to study her. He'd intended to focus on her face, but his gaze slipped past her dainty freckled nose and stubborn chin, then landed on her midriff. Hip-hugging jeans and a sleeveless crop top offered him an unfettered view of the dreaded belly ring. Heather sighed and the silver butterfly slipped below the waistband, then a moment later popped back into view, fluttering its wings.

"Royce!"

Jerking the steering wheel to the right, Royce swerved back into the proper lane. "Sorry," he grumbled. Good thing the roads were deserted this time of day. He'd better drag his mind out of the gutter if he expected the two of them to arrive at the ranch in one piece.

He opened his mouth to ask if she'd planned to finish earning her degree next fall, but stopped himself. The subject of Heather dropping her summer classes would only end in an argument. Even though he believed quarreling was the safest path to take with Heather, she didn't deserve to be provoked. "Luke will be happy to see you." His foreman was a safe topic. The aging cowboy had always had a soft spot for Heather.

"How's Luke doing?" Heather shifted against the seat, the movement sending a wave of honeysuckle-scented perfume his way.

"Ornery as ever. The arthritis is slowing him down some, so he doesn't work the cattle anymore. But he watches over the horses and weeds the vegetable garden."

She nibbled her lower lip, and he caught a glimpse of her crooked eyetooth. He'd always thought that tooth made her appear winsome when she smiled. She had pretty teeth. White and, except for the one tooth, remarkably straight for not having had braces.

"I've missed Luke, too." She fingered the stack of mayor-mail sitting on the seat between them. "Your life must be pretty hectic...being the mayor and playing cowboy."

He caught himself from blurting out that his life had become a lot less complicated the day she left for college. *And a lot more lonely.* "Do you remember the Wilkinson family?"

"The name sounds vaguely familiar."

"Their eldest son, Kenny, is sixteen now. He gives Luke a hand a couple of days a week. And every fall I pay several high school seniors to brand the cattle and get them ready to ship to market."

"What about the rest of the year?"

"I only run a few hundred head now. Most of the time, I manage fine on my own."

"Sounds like a lot of work for one man."

No argument there. By the end of the week he was exhausted. A year ago he'd thought about hiring another hand, but Luke had gotten all blustery and defensive and had insisted he could still lasso a cow. To prevent the old man from working himself into an early grave, Royce struggled along on his own and kept his mouth shut.

"Why did you decrease the size of your herd?"

"Beef prices aren't what they used to be. The first year after you graduated from high school, we suffered a drought. Four years later, I lost a hay crop to blister beetles. Ended up spending more money on cattle feed than what I got for the animals at market."

Heather's delicately arched eyebrows rose. "But things are better now?" Was it his imagination or did he hear genuine concern behind the question?

"We're back on our feet again." Not living in luxury, but the last of the loans and bills got paid off this past Christmas.

"If things were so tight, you shouldn't have sent me money."

Not once during her years away at college had Heather phoned or written him for money. He'd sent checks in her birthday cards, and Christmas cards, but she hadn't *asked* for a dime. "I wouldn't have given you the money if I couldn't have afforded to."

He turned off the county road and drove under a rickety wooden arch with the name Full Moon Ranch burned into the wood.

"The place hasn't changed much." Heather lowered her window, then stuck her head out.

With a critical eye, Royce studied the land. For once, the ruggedly beautiful terrain did not soothe him. Since his accident three years ago, things had lost their rosy glow. As the truck reached the top of a small incline, the east border of the property, which butted up against the towering pines of Atlanta State Park, came into view. To the west and north, he owned a thousand acres.

Two corrals, three outbuildings and the stereotypical red barn dotted the ranch yard. From this distance the gray, two-story house stood majestically beneath several sugar maple trees. But up close, the home lacked a grand appearance. The exterior hadn't been painted in twenty years and the sagging wraparound porch begged for tender, loving care. Except for new appliances and a television set for Luke's bedroom, nothing inside had been updated since he'd landed on his aunt and uncle's doorstep twenty-three years ago.

"Wow. Even the house is the same. Ever think about painting the place a different color? Maybe yellow with green shutters. Lots of Shasta daisies along the front and rosebushes by the steps would make the house more festive."

Festive was Heather's middle name. "If I have time this summer, I just might do that."

"I could lend a hand."

He conjured an image of Heather in cutoff jeans and a tank top, standing on a ladder, wielding a paintbrush. "You'll be too busy with the store."

As he pulled up to the house, he spotted Luke resting in the chair on the front porch, Bandit stretched out at his feet. Royce had lost count of the number of times he'd found the foreman and his useless dog snoozing away in the middle of the afternoon.

Aw, heck. He didn't care if Luke slept the whole day. After ten years of helping Royce with the ranch for little more than minimum wage, a bed and free meals, the old codger had more than earned his retirement.

Before Royce had even shifted the truck to park, Heather opened her door and hopped out. "Hi, Luke! Hi, Bandit!"

"Well, if you ain't the prettiest thing these ol' eyes have seen in a long time," Luke called as he shoved himself out of the chair and hobbled to the steps.

Heather met the foreman halfway.

With veiled envy, Royce watched Heather and Luke hug and laugh and smile at each other. Even the mangy dog got into the action, nudging Heather's hand with his head. She went down on one knee and ruffled the fleabag's fur as if they were long-lost friends. Her happiness at seeing Luke and his hound unsettled Royce. Three years ago she had wanted to spend the summer at his ranch, but his stubborn pride and aching heart had made sure she stayed away.

"Glad you're home, girl. I've missed you."

Royce slammed the truck door and approached the cozy circle. "Heather's decided to bunk at the store until the place sells."

"You didn't invite her to stay with us?" Luke scowled, then turned to Heather and added, "You're welcome to set up camp here. We got plenty of room."

Heather peeked at him and Royce swore her eyes twinkled in challenge. *No way.* He and Heather under the same roof was *not* a good idea. With Luke as a chaperone, he'd still have trouble keeping his hands off her. And his heart wouldn't stand a chance being near her day in and day out. When he looked at her he found it harder and harder to recall the image of the young teen he'd discovered crying outside her father's store. Replacing that tear-streaked face was a new image of a beautiful, courageous, determined woman. A woman he admired. A woman he hadn't stopped wanting for a very long time.

"Thanks for the offer, Luke. But Royce said the store requires major cleaning and repairs. I'll accomplish more if I stay there."

Stepping past the pair, Royce stomped up the porch steps. "I told her she could have the extra twin bed in the attic and the mini fridge in the barn."

"Want some help?" Her question followed him to the front door.

"No, thanks. I'm sure Miss Molly would appreciate a

visit from you." Luke called Bandit and the pair headed for the barn.

Heather stayed behind, a stricken expression in her eyes.

"What's the matter?" he asked.

"You still have Molly?"

Her question came out kind of wobbly, conveying how much the mare meant to her. He'd considered selling the horse a time or two, but never could do it. The tears in Heather's eyes made him fiercely glad he hadn't sold Molly or had her put down. "Go catch up with Luke. He'll fill you in on the mare."

A half hour later, Royce had the bed and mattress loaded into the back of the truck, along with fresh linens and a pillow. He didn't have a clue what Heather had packed in the boxes she'd brought with her. To be on the safe side, he'd gathered a few things he thought she might need—dishes, silverware, a reading light, a small coffeemaker, some dry food goods and bottled water. At the last minute he'd added laundry detergent, bath soap, shampoo, towels and a jumbo-size package of toilet paper.

He locked the tailgate, then headed down to the barn to ask if she wanted the Mustang—for pleasure, as she'd put it—right away. He hadn't started the car in a long while, and he expected the vehicle could use a tune-up before Heather got behind the wheel.

Royce entered the structure, then hesitated by the doors. As his eyes adjusted to the dim interior, the six empty horse stalls came into view. Just last week he'd moved the cutting horses to their summer grazing pasture south of the house.

The sound of soft laughter and murmuring voices drifted toward him from the back of the barn. He'd constructed an extra-large stall for Molly across from the tack room because he and Luke spent a lot of time there. Inside the stall he'd built a door that led to a small fenced-in pasture just for the horse. He moved quietly through the barn.

"You're still so pretty, Molly," Heather cooed. "I can't believe he didn't sell her, Luke."

Stopping, Royce shifted sideways until a beam concealed him. He didn't know what compelled him to eavesdrop.

"Sellin' Molly wasn't his decision, gal. She's your horse."

"I wondered from time to time if she missed her bedtime carrot."

Luke chuckled. "She didn't. Royce spoils her somethin' rotten. He made sure she got one."

"She's so skinny. Poor baby."

The catch in Heather's voice made Royce wish he could cure the mare. He figured seeing the sick horse would be difficult for her.

"Vet said she's got some kind of wastin' disease that there's no cure for. Still eats her fair share of oats and grain. And Royce planted a small alfalfa patch behind the barn for her."

"So, the big meanie spoils you, huh, Molly?"

Meanie? Royce had been called a lot of things in his life, but never a *meanie.*

"Is she in pain?"

"Nope. Just looks as if no one's fed her in months."

"How much longer does she have?" A sniffle followed Heather's question.

"Depends. Maybe another six months. When she gets too weak to stand, Royce'll call the vet."

"Oh, Molly. Such a sweet, sweet horse."

Royce couldn't bear the thought of Heather bursting into

tears, so he stepped out from behind his hiding place and cleared his throat as he approached the pair. "Molly's my star boarder." He stroked the mare's graying nose.

"Better get back to my garden. Them weeds ain't gonna hoe themselves," Luke grumbled as he shuffled away, Bandit on his heels.

Heather smiled at Royce. "Thank you for taking such good care of Molly."

"She was real sad when you left, Heather." Now, why had he gone and said something hurtful? Wasn't it enough she had to see her beloved horse wasting away? *You're a... a...meanie, McKinnon.*

"I'm glad I have a chance to spend some time with her before..." Heather's pretty blue eyes, glistening with tears, tugged at his heartstrings.

In the past, he'd always thought anger had caused her tears...but now he wondered if he hadn't misread her all those years ago. Before he realized his intent, he brushed a strand of blond hair from her cheek. "Visit her as often as you please."

"I remember the day you gave her to me. She was the best birthday gift I ever received."

He'd never regretted working the boat rental pier at Lake Wright that spring and most of that summer in order to buy the mare for Heather. She'd been deeply depressed the first year her mother had run off and he'd hoped the horse would lift her spirits.

Before things got too emotional, he suggested, "Let's take the tarp off the Mustang and see how she runs."

"DID YOU FLUNK OUT?"

Startled, Heather set aside the research articles she'd been reading for her term paper and grinned at her former high school classmate Amy Sanders. "No, I didn't flunk out."

The petite redhead's sandals clicked against the grainy wood floor as she strutted through the store. Her neon-green blouse and tight white miniskirt shouted size two from a mile away.

Heather hopped off the stool and moved out from behind the chipped Formica checkout counter.

"I can't imagine any other reason you'd come back to this ditch by the road." Amy opened her arms, and Heather bent to give her friend a warm hug.

"Nowhere isn't a bad place to live." Heather might have moved away, but she wasn't so closed minded that she didn't understand how others could appreciate this "ditch by the road" as her friend affectionately called the place. "I love your hair." Amy wore her bright red hair in a short, sassy style that emphasized her big brown eyes and pixielike features.

"Thanks. I'm a hairstylist at the Quick Curl over in Blairdsville." She lifted Heather's braid and frowned. "Still wearing your hair down to your butt, I see. When you're ready for a change, stop in at the salon and I'll cut your hair free."

"Thanks, I'll consider it."

"Crap, it's hot in this place." Amy fanned a hand in front of her face.

Flicking a bead of perspiration from her temple, Heather glanced at the ceiling. The newly cleaned fans whirred on low, barely stirring the humid, stagnant, smelling-of-compost-and-feed air inside the store. After she'd dragged the ladder from the storeroom and washed the blades, she'd discovered both the high and medium settings shook the fan so badly she feared the whole unit would drop right on a customer's head.

Amy rolled her eyes, then her elfin face sobered. "I'll say I'm sorry about your father if you want me to."

"Thanks, but that's not necessary." Heather hadn't believed Royce when he'd told her the good people of Nowhere had wanted to extend their sympathies on the death of her father. No one had liked or respected Melvin Henderson. Still, several of the town's merchants and residents had made a special trip into the store to offer a kind word and a welcome back.

"Okay, then spill your guts. If you didn't flunk out, why did you return home? Bobby Rae said you were supposed to graduate this year."

Did everyone in town know her business? Obviously, moving away from home didn't guarantee privacy. "I'm two courses short. I'd just signed up for summer school, then Royce called and..." She didn't want to talk about her father. "Anyway, I explained the situation to my professors and they agreed to let me complete the classes through correspondence." She scrunched her nose. "I have to write two monstrous papers by the end of the summer."

Rolling her eyes, Amy squealed, "Yuck!"

Yeah, yuck. Heather admitted she had doubts about her ability to run the store, finish her papers and find the answer to why Royce had cut her out of his life a few years back. Of the three, she suspected writing the papers would be the easiest.

Even Luke, who'd always been talkative, clammed up when she asked questions about Royce. Yesterday, she'd gone to visit Molly, and Luke had joined her in the barn. After a bit of chitchat she'd asked what Royce had done after he'd visited her at the university three years ago. Luke had avoided answering; instead, he'd mumbled that he had to see to his garden and had left the barn. Heather suspected something had happened that April long ago. Something no one wanted to talk about.

Amy hoisted herself onto the counter and crossed her legs. "I should be mad at you. I had to find out you were back in town from Bill at the gas station, who talked to Steve at the diner on Route 8, who ran into Mrs.—"

"Okay, okay." She squeezed Amy's arm. "I'm sorry I didn't call." She motioned to the doorway behind the counter. "I wanted to get settled in first."

"What do you mean, 'settled in'? I assumed you'd be staying out at the ranch with the *mayor.*" Amy grimaced as if saying the word made her ill. On a couple of occasions when Heather had gotten herself into deep horse hockey, Amy had been along for the ride. Her friend didn't pretend to have fond feelings for Royce.

"I fixed up the back room into a little apartment." At Amy's horrified expression she added, "Royce loaned me a bed, a small fridge, a hot plate and a coffeemaker. Everything I need." Along with a ton of extras he'd thoughtfully loaded in his truck the day he'd gotten the bed down from the attic for her. Heather was beginning to regret her bright idea to live in the back of the store. She'd thought Royce would check on her constantly, if only to try to convince her to sell, but he hadn't stopped in once since her return. She suspected he was avoiding her—a problem she'd have to fix soon.

"What about a shower?"

"There's a showerhead on the wall and a drain in the floor." After rearranging the supplies on all the shelves and cleaning the storage room yesterday, Heather had longed for a hot soak in a tub and had barely resisted the urge to drive out to Royce's ranch and ask if she could borrow his bathroom for two hours.

"C'mon, Heather. The store's a *dump*. Why are you really back in Nowhere?"

"I'm hoping that if I fix the place up I'll get more money for it." If Amy figured out why Heather had returned to Nowhere, she'd spread the word faster than a wildfire and Heather would never find out the truth. When the locals had welcomed her back, she'd asked a couple of general questions about what had gone on in the town in the past, but no one mentioned anything having to do with Royce, except that he'd run for mayor.

"What did the mayor say?" Amy asked.

"He wasn't happy about it."

Amy grinned. "Yeah, I bet."

During the days following Heather's decision to manage the store, Royce had phoned repeatedly and demanded she stay put. Even now, she shivered at the memory of hanging up on him and turning off the ringer on her cell phone. From then on, he'd left messages on her voice mail, which she'd promptly deleted without listening to them.

Amy hopped off the counter and turned in a slow circle, her eyes studying every inch of the store. "Are you sure you want to do this?"

"For now, yes."

"At least the store is easy. I'd hate to be in charge of something—" Amy waved a hand in front of her face "—busy."

Heather's stomach tightened. Waiting on customers, placing orders and doing inventory had been a breeze—because there wasn't much of any of that going on. Figuring out her father's shabby bookkeeping, worrying about the quarterly taxes that were due soon and the dismal sales for the month of June were enough to stress anyone out.

"I have to get back to the beauty shop. Mrs. Beuller is due for her Friday rinse. Thank God for blue-haired grannies—they keep us in business." At the door, Amy stopped. "The gang's getting together Saturday night at the Steer Dance Hall. Drop by. Everyone will be there."

Heather longed for some excitement and she missed socializing with friends. "I'll think about it." As if she'd just been zapped by a crack of lightning, she added with a smile, "Okay, I'll go."

"Great."

As soon as the door shut behind her friend, Heather snapped her fingers in excitement. After a few beers, some shots, everyone would loosen up and spill their guts. She'd find someone at the Steer who would recall what Royce had been up to three summers ago.

With that problem solved, Heather returned to her stool behind the counter. If she didn't find a way to pay all the taxes, she'd have to sell—and then what excuse would she use to stay in Nowhere the rest of the summer?

Math wasn't one of her best subjects in school, but even she understood the significance of all the red ink smeared across the store's financial records, which Royce had handed over the day she'd returned. She suspected the drop in revenue over the past several years had been due in part to locals purchasing supplies from a new business, Tri-County Farm and Feed, which offered large-quantity discounts and free delivery, and in part to her father's addiction to gambling.

One way or another she had to devise a plan to bring in more business. Aside from Amy, only two other people had entered the store since it had opened at seven—a cowboy looking for a can of chew, and a fisherman wanting directions to Lake Wright.

Always the optimist, she believed that if she concentrated hard enough she'd find the answer. She grabbed her Rangers baseball cap from the hook on the wall and slapped it on her head. Whenever she felt unsettled, she wore the hat Royce had bought for her after he'd forced her to attend a Ranger game in Dallas, the summer of her sixteenth birthday. Of course she'd pretended she hated every minute of the experience, when in fact the opposite had been true. She'd loved the fans, the music and, best of all, the fireworks after each home run.

Pacing the store aisles, she studied the inventory. Most of the dust-coated products were self-explanatory. Corn feed. Horse halters. Foal feeder. Fencing nails. Salt and mineral blocks. But one item caught her attention. *Udder balm.* What did one do with udder balm? She lifted the lid and her nose curled at the odor. "Massage twice daily over the cow's udder to heal dry, cracked skin." Eeew!

She returned the jar to the shelf, stepped outside the store and sucked in a lungful of muggy summer air. Sitting down on the front stoop, chin on her palm, she stared across the street.

Thirty seconds of watching the red-and-white spinning stripes on the barbershop pole and she was ready to throw up. She pressed a hand to her queasy stomach and shifted her gaze to the newspaper stand at the corner. The *County Courier.*

Bingo!

Chapter Five

"What the hell is this?" Royce McKinnon demanded, as he stormed up the center aisle of the store. He smacked the *County Courier* against his muscular thigh, then tossed the newspaper on the counter in front of Heather. The paper landed with a *thud,* sending dust particles fluttering into the air.

Heather's heart skidded to a near stop, then kicked into overdrive. Blue eyes locked with brown eyes, but the retort on the tip of her tongue dangled unspoken. He hadn't been by the store once in the two weeks she'd been back. And the five times she'd visited the ranch he'd been conspicuously absent.

His scowl deepened, and his dark, slashing eyebrows lent him a sinister air, reminding her of a stagecoach robber in an old spaghetti western. Fascinated, she watched the muscle along his jaw pulse with anger.

He needed a shave. She curled her fingers into her palm, resisting the urge to test the prickliness of the reddish gold stubble. He removed his hat and the gray strands above his ears shimmered and sparkled in the late-afternoon sun that streamed through the store windows.

An enormous yearning tugged deep within her—the

same jittery longing she'd experienced the moment she'd spotted him in the church parking lot when she first arrived.

"Well?"

Startled by his growl, she shifted her attention to Saturday's edition of the *County Courier.* Hoping to soften his grumpiness, she flashed an impish smile and feigned an air of innocence. "Well, what?"

He pointed to the ad circled in red ink. "Explain this."

"What's to explain? The ad is perfectly clear."

"You can't be serious."

He leaned forward, crowding her. He meant to intimidate, but she wondered what he'd think if he knew how badly she wanted to press her mouth against the rugged lips inches from hers. *Probably have a heart attack.* A whiff of cologne drifted under her nose and she inhaled deeply, the scent nicer than anything she'd smelled the entire day.

A flicker of anger at Royce's bossiness ignited her temper. Determined to keep her cool, she swallowed a sarcastic reply. "Royce." The husky catch in her voice seemed to shock him more than her. His eyes narrowed as she cleared her throat. "I don't want to argue."

The lines bracketing his mouth relaxed. "Why didn't you contact me before you did this?"

"And when would I have had the chance to tell you? You haven't dropped in since I returned to town, and when I visit Molly you're off playing with your cows somewhere."

A flush spread across his cheekbones. "You could have phoned."

"I suppose, but why bother? You would have tried to change my mind."

"Hell yes. This is the most ridiculous—"

"Oh, really?" As a rule, Heather considered herself even

tempered and slow to anger. But Royce made her mad enough to spit the fencing staples in aisle four.

"You should have discussed this with me."

"I'm twenty-five years old. I don't need to discuss *anything* with you." She straightened her shoulders and felt a zing of satisfaction when his glare dropped to the hint of cleavage showing above her navy spandex top. He wasn't as immune to her as he'd have her believe. As a matter of fact, feminine instinct told her that Royce was still very much attracted to her, although he seemed determined to deny it.

As if he had nothing better to do with his day than harass her, he moved the paper aside, then leaned one hip against the counter and folded his arms over his chest. "Why are you doing this?"

Might as well get right to the point or he'd stand there until moss grew around his boot heels. "I've got a little over a week to come up with the money to pay the quarterly taxes due the end of June."

"And this is your answer?"

"Yes." At least she hoped to make enough money to meet the tax bill.

"Sell the store and go back to college. For once, finish something you start and earn your degree." He straightened, obviously believing he had the last word on the situation. "In the meantime, withdraw the ad and write a retraction for the paper."

She would not let him bully her into giving up and leaving town. "No. I will not." Lifting her chin, she hoped to add another inch to her five-eight height. For all the good it did. He still towered over her.

Hands braced on the counter, he shoved his muscular

chest in her face. The top two snaps of his western shirt popped open and the seams pulled at the shoulders. Unable to drag her gaze away from the thatch of russet hair peeking through the opening, she licked her dry lips.

He mumbled a curse, stormed several feet away, then faced her. His challenging glare differed from the glares he'd given her in the past when she'd gotten herself in a mess. This one was... *Sexual.*

Flustered, and feeling the slightest bit naughty, she pursed her lips and blew a kiss in his direction.

His head jerked back as if the air kiss had smacked him in the face. "You're still a handful, Heather." He spun away, boot heels clomping against the floor. When he reached the door, his hand hesitated on the knob. "If you don't take care of the ad, I will." The threat hung heavy in the air.

"Royce?"

Glowering over his shoulder, he growled, "What?"

"Could I interest you in a fence post?"

"What the heck do I need a fence post for?"

"Why, to shove it up your—"

The bell above the door jingled, followed by a slam that threatened to bring the store's rotting walls crumbling to the ground.

Okay, so they hadn't gotten off to a great start since she'd returned to Nowhere. *Stubborn. Mulish. Obstinate man.* She lifted the paper from the counter and read the advertisement again.

> Local lottery. Purchase $100 worth of merchandise from Henderson Feed Store and receive lottery ticket for drawing held last Saturday of June. Prize:

Collector's Edition 1969 Mustang Convertible. Canary yellow. Deluxe white interior. 390 engine.

For the past two nights, she'd tossed in bed, agonizing over the idea of giving away her beloved Mustang. The decision hadn't been made lightly. She suspected she'd probably get more for the car if she sold it through one of those fancy car magazines. But that kind of ad required a lot of cash, which she didn't have. Mr. Mahooney, the editor of the *County Courier,* had given her the advertising space free as a "welcome home" gesture.

Guilt struck Heather hard and heavy. The Mustang meant as much to Royce as it did to her. She'd saved her waitress wages for over two years, then Royce had taken her out to shop for a vehicle. He'd recommended the economy models, but as soon as she'd seen the sporty, yellow Mustang with the beautiful white leather seats her heart had melted.

Royce had dickered for over an hour with the owner, until the man had dropped two thousand dollars off the price. But Heather still hadn't had enough money. Claiming his contribution had been an early birthday present from him, Royce had made up the difference.

He'd spent a lot of time showing her how to care for the car—change the oil, replace a flat tire—things her own father hadn't offered to do. She'd lost track of the number of Sunday afternoons she and Royce had washed and waxed the Mustang at his ranch.

Over the years, the car seemed to be the one thing that had eased the tension between them. Was she a fool to get rid of it?

LUKE GRINNED around the wad of chew bulging against his cheek. "She done twisted your boxers, didn't she."

"My boxers are fine." Scowling, Royce approached the corral where Luke watched Heather's mare, Molly, prance and dance for his stallion, Hank.

Eyes twinkling with laughter, Luke motioned to the animals. "Molly's got the hots for Hank."

Royce snorted. "The mare ought to know better at her age."

Rubbing his whiskered jaw, the foreman studied Royce. "Heather's a right pretty gal. She got a young feller friend?"

"Not that I'm aware of." The thought of Heather with another man made his chest burn. And he wouldn't call her *pretty,* either. *Stunning, breathtaking, gorgeous* better described the thorn in his side. If he allowed his thoughts to wander, he could spend all day thinking about her clear blue eyes and how his hands ached to unbraid her long blond hair.

Luke cleared his throat and set a boot on the bottom rail. "Ever since you come back from the university, you ain't been yourself."

Now, what in the heck is that supposed to mean? "You never miss a good opportunity to shut up, do you."

Grinning, his foreman teased, "If the year were 1876, you could just take a trip to town and scratch your itch with a local saloon girl."

Since the accident, Royce never admitted to himself, except on rare occasions that he hadn't been particularly satisfied with his love life these past couple of years. There were moments when he felt so alone. When life seemed too predictable. Too boring.

Heather. Life with her would never be predictable, boring or empty. He shoved the thought aside. "I didn't ask for advice about my sex life, you meddling coot."

"Someone's gotta watch out for you. One day your handsome mug'll turn sour."

Royce grinned. "You think so?"

"Ain't nothin' funny, boy." Luke sobered. "You got serious feelings for the gal, don't you."

"It's none of your business." He started to leave, but paused when Luke's gnarled fingers grabbed his shirtsleeve.

"I figured somethin' had happened between the two of you that time you visited her at the university." He released Royce's shirt. "Is it because of the accident that you never went back to see Heather?"

A sharp pain sliced through Royce, making it difficult for him to breathe. "What's done is done, Luke." He rubbed a hand across his shirtfront, hoping to ease the hurt that was always present when he reflected on the past.

"So, you just goin' to forget about her?"

"Something like that."

"I may be old, but I ain't simple. You're a fool if you let that one slip off the hook." Shaking his head, the bowlegged cowpoke ambled toward the house.

Royce waited several minutes until the pain settled into a dull throb and he was finally able to draw in a deep breath. Needing a little space, he decided to muck out Molly's stall, but twenty minutes later he still couldn't get Heather off his mind. He kicked the pile of dirty hay in front of him, then cursed at the fresh turd clinging to the tip of his Laredo boot.

For the past week, he'd avoided checking up on the little businesswoman, determined to step out of the way and not interfere with her ridiculous crusade to save the feed store. Then she'd placed the ad in the paper for her cockamamy *lottery* idea. Although he'd never tell her, his first reaction after having read the ad was, *What a brilliant idea.*

Sure, he'd been ticked that she'd even consider selling the Mustang. He had a lot of fond memories of her, him and the car. But what bothered him most was the possibility that the lottery might be a success. If Heather managed to pay the quarterly taxes, she'd stick around. He didn't think—no, he knew—he didn't have the strength to avoid her for another month.

Deciding a cold shower would brighten his mood, he finished loading the last pile of horse dung into the wheelbarrow. Back at the house, he removed his stinky boots, then set them in the corner of the utility room and entered the kitchen. A cold brew waited inside the fridge, but he passed it up and headed for the bathroom. He'd shower, then return to town and have another go at convincing Heather to drop the lottery idea.

Upstairs in the bedroom he emptied his pockets and set his wallet on the dresser next to another copy of the *County Courier.* Twelve more copies lay scattered on the floor of his truck. When he'd seen the ad, he'd bought every last paper in the vending box outside the barbershop. The fewer people who heard about the lottery, the better.

Relief from the cold shower didn't last long. A gust of hot, humid air hit Royce square in the face when he left the house twenty minutes later. Cursing the bead of sweat rolling down his temple, he got in the truck and slammed the door. His hand hesitated on the ignition key when he caught a glimpse of himself in the rearview mirror. The accident had aged him. He'd like to blame the tiny lines fanning out from the corners of his eyes on years spent in the sun, but he couldn't.

He tilted his head and winced at the number of gray hairs in his hair. He hadn't had a single gray hair three years ago. Shattered dreams had a way of marking a man.

Enough foolishness. After starting the motor, he shifted into gear and headed for town. He drove into the delivery driveway behind the feed store, then slammed on the brakes. The Mustang was missing. *Now what is she up to?*

The only place he knew of that young adults around Nowhere went after eight p.m. on a Saturday night was the dance hall called the Steer. He wasn't in the mood for dancing tonight. Ten minutes later he pulled off the highway into a dirt parking lot. And there, smack dab in front of the building's entrance, sat the yellow Mustang.

He parked in the back row, then headed toward the group of wannabe cowboys with baby-faced skin, running their hands over the surface of the Mustang as they inspected the car from bumper to bumper. Royce stopped next to the tailpipe. "At your age I was feeling up girls, not cars."

The crowd snickered and one of the young men stepped forward. "Howdy, Mayor. We were just admirin' the lottery prize." The rednecks guffawed.

"Forget the lottery. It's been canceled."

A discontented rumble echoed in the evening air. "Now, get. Before I call each of your parents and ask your age."

Half the crowd dispersed in the parking lot; the other half returned to the bar. Satisfied no one would bother the Mustang, Royce entered the honky-tonk.

"Good evening, Mayor. ID?" The six-foot-one three-hundred-pound lineman for the University of Texas held out his hand expectantly.

"You're joking, right, Rodney?"

The bouncer's eyes rounded. "How'd you know my name, sir?"

"Your mother calls me every year to ride in the Blairdsville parade."

Two meaty fingers snapped in front of Royce's nose. "Oh, yeah. You drive that yellow Mustang out front."

"I'm not here to socialize. I'm searching for someone."

Rodney's brow furrowed. "Sorry, Mayor. Gotta card everyone." He leaned forward and whispered, "It's the law."

Muttering an oath, Royce fished his wallet from the back pocket of his jeans and slid his license out.

"Go right ahead, Mayor."

Scowling, he handed the gorilla a five-dollar bill for the cover charge and entered the bar through a second set of doors. The air pulsed with a pounding bass rhythm as the band's guitar player stroked out a solo on stage. Nose itching from a combination of cloying perfume, cigarette smoke, sweat and spilled beer, he stood against the back wall until his eyesight adjusted to the dark interior and strobe lights.

The crowded dance floor—filled with fast-moving bodies and flying hair—made finding Heather next to impossible. He focused on the bar, where a group had gathered.

Figured. Heather stood in the center of the circle, surrounded by males and females vying for her attention. Like a queen paying court to her subjects, she smiled, touched and hugged every blasted person within ten feet of her.

Tonight her hair was down. Way down. The dark blond locks shimmered each time the lights from the stage flashed across the bar area. Royce caught his breath when she flung her head back, laughing at something the idiot next to her had said. Her hair skimmed her waist and swayed softly. *Oh, man.* Remembering how his fingers had threaded through those long strands when he'd kissed her made his jeans uncomfortable.

Frowning, he watched the young stud move in on Heather. The pansy swaggered like a preening cock—brand-new cowboy hat, shiny, scuff-free boots and jeans with a crease sharp enough to split the skin. He trusted the guy about as much as he trusted a newly weaned calf not to follow its mama.

The stud snuck an arm around Heather's waist and Royce clenched his hands into fists. His knee-jerk adolescent reaction startled him. He wasn't in high school anymore and Heather wasn't his girl.

She offered the cowboy a friendly—too friendly, in Royce's opinion—smile, then conversed with a petite, redheaded woman who reminded him of the young troublemaker Heather had hung out with in high school.

When the cowboy's hand inched higher, Royce swore the smile on Heather's face tightened. He shoved away from the wall and circled the crowd, never taking his eyes off her and *the hand.* He'd only made it halfway across the room, when the jerk slid his palm over her fanny.

Hellfire!

What he wouldn't give to be wearing his cow-manure-encrusted boots so he could stomp the fingers clean off the dandy's hand. When the guy's grip flexed against her hip pocket, he changed his route and cut across the dance floor, breaking up couples in his way. Never before had he felt such a loss of control. Heather Henderson turned him every which way but the right direction.

As he approached the group, the redhead's eyes widened and he heard her gasp before she snagged the elbow of a nearby cowboy and dragged him onto the dance floor. The others parted like a stampede around an angry rattler, leaving him face-to-face with Heather and the Slick Mick.

He pinned the young cowboy with a nasty glare. "Take your hand off her ass."

Heather's mouth sagged open.

Raising his arms in the air, the guy backed up. "Hey, man. I don't want any trouble."

Royce moved forward and the stud lost himself in the crowd. *Chicken.*

Angry sparks lit Heather's blue eyes. But before she could squawk a single protest, he tugged her toward the exit. They almost made it to the door before she dug her heels in. It was either stop or drag her the rest of the way. He stopped.

"How dare—"

"Not now." He flung open the door. With a firm hand against her back, he guided her out of the bar.

Rodney's eye's widened. "Problem, Mayor?"

"Problem's leaving." He followed Heather out the door and into the parking lot, grateful she hadn't put up a bigger fuss. He grinned at the outrage on her face.

Compared with some of his rescues during her teen years, tonight's had been relatively easy and painless.

Chapter Six

"I didn't realize you made a habit of abducting women from bars." The effort to keep her voice emotionless strained Heather's nerves.

The muscle along Royce's jaw tightened, then relaxed, then tightened, then relaxed… Good grief! What had she done to tick him off now? She racked her brain to come up with a reason but drew a blank.

Grasping her upper arm, he led her to the Mustang, opened the driver's door and pressed down on her shoulder until she sat on the seat. "I'll follow you back to the store."

In the nick of time she snatched her arm away before the door slammed on her elbow. *Big bully.* She clutched the wheel but didn't insert the key into the ignition. Staring—rather, glaring—at him, she counted to ten, determined not to throw a hissy fit in front of the small crowd gathering outside.

If the occasion warranted, she could be as mature and rational as the next person. "I have no idea what I've done to upset you. Regardless, I don't deserve to be dragged around by the hair like some prehistoric cave woman." Satisfaction surged through her when his face reddened and he slid his gaze away.

"We can have this discussion right here—"

He motioned to the bar with his head, and Heather noticed the group of onlookers had doubled.

"Or we can go back to the store. Your call."

Tomorrow, rumors of the mayor abducting her would travel clear across the county…maybe even over the state line into Arkansas. She glanced at the nosy yahoos. "I'll see you at the store." She turned the key, shifted in reverse and stomped on the accelerator. Royce stumbled to get out of the way and almost fell on his nice, hard, perfect butt.

In the rearview mirror she watched him stomp to his truck, angrier than a bear with a bee sting. His mood reminded her of the afternoon he'd stormed into her apartment and started an argument over her having changed majors again.

When she'd asked how he'd known that, he'd set the forwarded letter on her table. Evidently, the school hadn't updated her records with her new address and had sent the schedule change to her emergency contact—Royce. At first she'd been miffed that he'd opened the letter from the university, but seeing how their argument had ended…

After Royce had gotten over his initial shock when she'd planted that first kiss on his lips to shush him, he'd initiated the second kiss. And then the third. The fourth. His kisses had been wild, fast, hard, exhilarating. Then something had changed and his mouth had softened, cherished and worshiped hers until she'd stopped counting his kisses.

Anticipation hummed through her blood as she sped down the rural road. The sultry Texas night stirred up fantasies of her and Royce alone in the store, and they sure weren't talking!

In retrospect, she was relieved he'd put an end to her night out on the town. She'd arrived at the Steer a little over an hour earlier, and before long the excitement of seeing old friends had worn off. After the initial barrage of questions and chitchat she'd realized how much she'd changed over the past seven years and how little everyone else had. The group reminisced about the old days as if they'd happened last week, and no one appeared worried about the future, world affairs, saving the rain forest or the recent floods in California that threatened several communities.

She'd made a few inquiries about Royce, the town and what events had taken place three years ago, but no one remembered anything unusual happening. Amy thought she'd heard through the grapevine that Royce had been dating a local divorced teacher on and off, but the woman had moved away over a year ago.

By nine o'clock she'd decided the evening had been a bust. Then Fast Hands had stuck his fingers into her jeans pocket. He'd asked her to dance several times, but she'd declined. So the dummy had asked for a date. When she'd politely refused, he'd offered to show her his truck. Talk about dense!

Speaking of annoying people… Royce flashed his high beams at her. Probably wanted to make sure she didn't miss the turnoff. Her ire rose, then she reminded herself to behave like an adult—though that didn't mean she couldn't goad his temper a bit.

She took the corner on two wheels.

Laughter erupted from her as she pictured the scowl on his face at the daring maneuver. She decreased her speed when she came into town, then parked behind the store and went in through the back entrance. As the door closed, the sound of Royce's truck echoed down Main Street.

After flicking on the lights, she grabbed two long-necks out of the mini fridge, twisted off the caps, then sat Indian-style on the back counter and waited.

Two minutes later, the clomp of boot heels against the cement floor echoed in the storeroom. The clomping halted for a moment, and she assumed he'd stopped outside her living quarters to check for her. More clomping, until he appeared in the doorway.

His muscular shoulders blocked the light behind him, casting his shadow across the floor. The front of the store, lit only by a neon Purina Dog Chow sign in the front window and the street lamp at the corner, created a cozy, intimate atmosphere.

His gaze went from her to the second bottle of beer, which sat on the counter by her hip. After a slight hesitation, he moved forward and reached for the drink.

Her nerves jumped as she lifted her bottle to his in an unspoken toast. Aware his eyes followed her every move, she brought the bottle to her mouth. The smooth malt flavor cooled her parched throat. A drop of amber liquid escaped, and she licked the bead from her lower lip.

His nostrils flared. His eyes narrowed. His shoulders stiffened. *Yeah, things were progressing nicely.*

A trickle of perspiration rolled between her breasts as the room closed in around them. Never taking her gaze off his face, she rubbed the sweating bottle against the flushed skin exposed above her low-cut T-shirt. Back and forth…slowly.

Hypnotized, Royce followed the bottle with his eyes.

Her breasts tingled.

Afraid she'd melt under his fiery stare, she asked, "What

was so urgent you had to crash the party and ruin my evening?" Did that husky voice belong to her?

He ignored her question, finished off his beer, then set the bottle on the counter with a clunk. Feeling mischievous, she crossed her arms under her breasts, raising them a good two inches. The scowl slid right off his face.

"What the hell kind of outfit is that?" His words might not be a compliment, but the way his gaze devoured her was.

She glanced at herself. "What do you mean?"

"You like showing off your…" He pointed a finger in the direction of her chest.

Obviously, he suffered from a limited vocabulary. "Breasts?"

"Every rutting male within a hundred miles will be sniffing after you."

"Might bring in more business—for the store, I mean."

Sputtering, he slapped his thigh in frustration. "That's another thing. The store."

Shoot. She should have kept her mouth shut. "What about it?" Watching a normally cool, composed man morph into a discombobulated nut was rather entertaining.

"This lottery thing you started…" He shook his head. "Stupid idea."

"What—?"

He held up a hand. "Hear me out. The lottery is nothing but a quick fix."

"I'm well aware of that." She didn't appreciate the insinuation that she hadn't given the idea considerable thought. She had.

"You've got major financial problems with the business. A few thousand dollars won't help in the long run. You still have two years' worth of taxes to pay off."

True. Shifting, she dangled her legs over the counter. "What do you suggest?"

He pivoted on his boot heel and began to pace back and forth. "Sell."

"There's just one problem with selling."

"What's that?"

"Then I'll have no reason to stay in Nowhere."

He stopped mid-stride, then turned, his face devoid of emotion. "Why would you want to stay here?"

"Because of you."

A noise that reminded her of a wounded animal escaped through the space between his lips. His eyes flashed with heat, but he said nothing.

"You want to know the real reason I came back here?"

He looked everywhere but at her. "No."

"I'll tell you anyway. I came home to get some answers."

His shoulders sagged, as if he understood he was the only person who could provide the answers to her questions. He rubbed a hand across the back of his neck and shifted his gaze to her face.

Now that she had his attention, she wasn't sure she was brave enough to ask the question. Clenching her fingers into a tight fist, she forced the words past her lips. "I deserve to know why you kicked me out of your life three years ago after we kissed."

He winced, as if talking about the past was too painful. "We kissed. Big deal, Heather." He added in a much quieter voice. "It was a mistake."

Was he apologizing or just stating a fact? "A mistake? I don't think so. And you're a liar if you say your heart wasn't involved."

"Don't do this, Heather."

The despair in his glazed eyes convinced her that something had occurred after Royce had left her apartment that afternoon…something that had changed his mind about her. About them. “It’s not like you to be dishonest, Royce.”

“Let it go.”

An ache filled her at the desperation in his voice. Why wouldn’t he trust her? “I can’t,” she whispered. The man was so obstinate she knew they could argue for months on end and not resolve anything. She picked at the label on the beer bottle, piling the shredded paper on the counter.

“You always were a willful person.”

She crinkled her nose. “Takes one to know one.” She wondered how to convince Royce to trust her enough to share whatever deep dark secret he was hiding. Time to drop the subject. Right now she wanted to feel his breath whisper across her cheek. Feel the pressure of his hand on the small of her back—not shoving her through a door, but coaxing her nearer. Feel his mouth on hers.

“Cancel the lottery, Heather.”

Cajoling a kiss out of the cowboy might be more difficult than she’d expected. She hopped off the counter, swallowing a chuckle when he scooted back. “I don’t want to talk about the lottery.”

“I’ve always looked out for you,” he insisted, as if words would somehow act as a barrier between them.

“Yes, you have.” With her eyes she stalked him. With her feet she inched forward. “But you need to understand that I can handle my own life.”

He snorted, then retreated another step. His leg bumped a pyramid of metal feed buckets, knocking them over and creating an ear-piercing din.

Ignoring the mess, she concentrated on the tingling sensation setting her skin on fire. She was tired of discussing. Tired of thinking. She just wanted to *feel.* One more step.

His back hit the wall.

She had him right where she wanted him. *Trapped.* Sliding her palm up his chest and over his shoulder, she curled her fingers around his neck.

Their breath mingled. Her lips throbbed as she narrowed the gap between their mouths…inch by inch. She expected him to resist, but he surprised her by tilting his head and bringing their mouths in contact.

His lips were warm, a little rough and so wonderfully male.

She sipped at his lips until he relaxed against her. Then she ran the tip of her tongue across his lower lip. A rumble vibrated through his chest. His mouth parted, and she snuck her tongue inside. He tasted of beer and desire. Something dark and dangerous…Royce's own masculine flavor. He didn't kiss her back, but for one infinitesimal second his body shuddered with need…a need for her.

After a never-ending moment, she broke the kiss and gulped a lungful of air. Trying to balance herself on wobbly legs, she dug her fingers into his biceps. The kiss had left her thoroughly sated, weak and vulnerable. And she'd been the one doing all the kissing!

Fingers biting into her, he demanded, "Why the hell did you do that?"

Because you're too stubborn to take what you desperately want—me. He might act as if he didn't care for her anymore, as if what they'd shared once upon a time meant nothing to him, but his dark brown eyes said otherwise. He'd wanted her kiss as badly as she'd wanted his.

Dropping his hand from her hip, he edged away from

the wall and retreated around the counter. He paused at the doorway to the storeroom. "No more kissing, Heather."

"No more promises, Royce."

FEELING OLDER than his thirty-two years, and stinking worse than an outhouse on a humid day, Royce steered the truck toward the corrals and glanced at his watch. He'd wasted the whole day coddling a bunch of irascible cows, because he couldn't keep his mind on the task at hand. Heather had a way of messing with a man's concentration.

The kiss she'd planted on him a week ago after he'd rescued her from the cowboy-with-a-thousand-hands was as clear as the cloudless blue sky above.

After living off nothing but memories the past few years, the taste of her mouth and the feel of her against him had brought the past rushing at him like an NFL defensive line. Her kiss had cut his legs right out from under him. For the past week, he'd been plagued by dreams of making love to Heather, followed by nightmares of the accident and the painful phone call weeks later when he'd broken things off with her.

Exorcising Heather from his thoughts was easier said than done. He'd worked from sunup to sundown, until his body screamed with exhaustion. If he could just keep his distance until she gave up and left Nowhere. He admitted his strength took a nasty blow each time he got a glimpse of her. She'd burrowed under his skin worse than a deer tick. If he wasn't careful, she'd catch him off guard and he'd bare his soul to her.

He shifted into park, then pulled the key from the ignition. As he studied the house, he admitted Heather had been right. The sunflower yellow he'd painted the outside gave the place a downright cheery feel. Luke had stripped the shutters and Royce planned to paint them grass green to-morrow.

Slipping from the truck, he winced as a bolt of pain shot up his spine. Instead of having let a mama cow rescue her own baby from the tangled vine along the fence earlier in the day, he'd jumped in to help free the small calf. While he'd attempted to cut the vine away from the animal's back legs, the little troublemaker had head-butted him in the chest, sending him flying. His back end had landed smack-dab in a pile of cow crap the size of a Frisbee.

Now, smelling ranker than rotting roadkill and feeling tired as hell, he walked gingerly toward the house, deter-mined to drown any lingering thoughts of Heather in a long, cold shower and a few beers—not necessarily in that order. As he neared the porch he heard the faint growl of a motor. A cloud of dust billowed in the air as a truck headed toward the house. *Heather?*

Someone should just shoot him and put him out of his misery.

He waited until the old, beat-up Ford drew closer. An inch of grime covered the front windshield, and he won-dered how she could see the road, never mind two feet in front of her. Melvin Henderson should have sold the piece of scrap metal years ago.

He didn't want her here. Not today. Not tomorrow. Not ever.

Being around Heather was like tossing his emotions into a blender and flipping the switch to puree. Genuine concern for her welfare, physical desire for her and guilt played havoc with his blood pressure and nervous system. The more he saw her the more he wished for things that couldn't be.

Hopping out of the driver's side, she flashed a smile brighter than the late-afternoon sun. He went a little soft inside when he saw the messy blond ponytail sticking out the back of her Rangers baseball cap. The fact that she'd kept the hat made him more sad than happy.

She sashayed around the hood, then stopped abruptly. "Wow, the house looks great."

If he hadn't been leaning against the porch banister he'd have fallen flat on his backside a second time today. The bright pink top with spaghetti straps left visible a good four inches of tanned, trim tummy…and that sexy little butterfly attached to her belly button. He hated like hell to admit it, but the belly ring was growing on him.

His gaze slid lower, taking in the frayed edges of her denim shorts. Confident the mirrored glasses concealed his interest, he studied her sleek, tanned legs. What little there was of the shorts gloved her round fanny to perfection. *Holy cripes.* He imagined the geezers in town were still searching for their dentures after she'd sauntered by the barbershop window.

Crossing his arms over his chest, he grumbled, "What's wrong now?"

For a second her smile faltered, then she turned up the wattage. "My, my. Aren't we grumpy." She slid her fingers into her back pockets, and he swore the little butterfly fluttered its wings at him.

He was in trouble. Big trouble. He glanced at the sky, praying the heavens would crash down around him and end all this. "I've had a hell of a day. If this is a social call, I'm not in the mood."

"I'm delivering the order Luke phoned in."

Blast it, Luke.

His foreman was determined to see Heather succeed even if it sent Royce into bankruptcy. Luke had placed enough orders over the past five days to supply three ranches through the end of the year. "Who's watching the store?"

"No one. I put a yellow sticky note on the door and left the ledger on the counter."

Was she crazy? "You expect people to write down what they take and leave their money?" Hadn't he taught her better?

"If they don't stop back to pay up in a few days, I'll send a bill."

She studied him and he felt like a bug caught between a pair of tweezers.

"You're such a pessimist."

Great. Now she was putting her psychology courses to work on him. "You're too trusting."

She gestured toward the house. "May I come in?"

Evidently, they were through discussing her business practices. "No." He tromped up the steps. His house was the only place left that gave him any peace—except at night when he went to bed and couldn't get *her* out of his head.

She bounced past him, like some beboppin' cheerleader.

Brat. He dogged her heels, sniffing the light, honeysuckle scent floating in her wake. She propped the screen door open with her foot. Pink toenails winked at him through the straps of her sandals. Heather ought to know better than to haul around fifty-pound sacks of feed in that flimsy footwear.

Once inside the kitchen, she went straight to the refrigerator and opened the door.

"Help yourself," he muttered as she eyed the contents.

"Here." She held out a soda.

He'd rather have a beer. Annoyed, he accepted the can, popped the top and downed the drink. "Since when does Henderson Feed Store deliver orders?" He removed his sunglasses and set them on the table.

"Since today. I drove over to Tri-County Farm and Feed and talked with the manager last week. He suggested I try free delivery to increase sales."

"He did, huh." Royce pressed his lips together to keep from asking if she'd worn that same outfit when she'd talked to the manager of the chain store.

"Bob said—"

"Who's Bob?"

"The manager of Tri-County. Anyway, Bob said people today want personal service."

"Is that right." He hated the way she said *Bob*—like they were longtime friends…or something more.

She selected a soda for herself and shut the fridge door. "Bob said people will pay more for a product if it's less hassle."

"Really?"

"Bob believes good service will build loyalty and keep customers coming back."

She was beginning to sound like an annoying TV commercial. "Bob sure is smart."

A frown marred her pretty face. "You don't think free delivery is a good idea?"

"I don't think leaving the store unattended is a good idea."

"Not to worry." She waved a hand dismissively. "You're my only delivery today."

Didn't she have an ounce of common sense? "What if business picks up and you're out delivering orders all day?"

Guilt nagged him. He shouldn't be so hard on her. Heather might not understand much about running a business, but unlike her father, she was giving it her all.

"If orders pick up, I'll hire someone to watch the store."

She had a knack of making everything sound so simple. "Where will you get the money to pay for extra help?"

One eyebrow arched.

"What?" he asked.

"You've always been one of those people who view the glass half empty instead of half full."

"There's nothing wrong with being cautious."

Her lips curved in a catlike smile as she edged closer. Suddenly the air in the room thinned and his lungs squeezed painfully with each breath. The kitchen table was behind him. He had nowhere to escape to, unless he wanted to make a fool of himself and run out the back door. Which he just might do if her perky little breasts got much closer to his chest.

"Caution is good. But it's not a very exciting way to live." She flicked a speck of dried dirt from his shirtsleeve.

At least, he hoped the brown stuff was dirt and not manure. He opened his mouth to warn her, but her eyes widened and she gasped, then stumbled backward. He reached for her, but she shook her head and moved to the other side of the room.

Pinching her nose, she squeaked, "You stink."

"No kidding." Neck heating, Royce shifted away.

"I like hardworking men, but…"

He was hard, all right.

She had that look in her eye—the same hungry, yearning, needy look she'd had the night he'd abducted her from the Steer. Her eyes froze him in place as she edged toward him again. She stopped in front of him—obviously, his smell didn't bother her anymore—and tapped a finger against his belt buckle. "I don't remember you ever wearing a rodeo buckle before."

He sidestepped so fast he careered into the table, knocking it up on two legs before it came crashing down.

"I rodeoed the summer I graduated from high school."

Her soft chuckle grated on his nerves. "What did you ride…bulls or broncs?"

Damn her. She was messing with him again. He set his hands on her shoulders and forced some distance between them. "It's not going to work, Heather."

"What?"

"Trying to come on to me."

Her lower lip pouted. "You're attracted to me."

Sliding past her, he went to stare out the window over the sink. He was tired of pretending. Tired of lying. "I do want you."

"Then why are you avoiding me?"

Tell her. Just blurt out the hard, cold facts and be done with it. "It's personal and private and something I don't want to share with you."

"So, kissing me that afternoon in my apartment three years ago meant nothing to you?"

"I didn't say that—" His voice broke and he hated himself for letting his emotions leak into the conversation.

The stillness in the kitchen turned heavy and suffocating. "Was there another woman?"

Her quiet question caused an ache in his chest. He yearned to say yes, but he owed her something for how badly he'd handled the past. "No. I wasn't dating anyone then."

"What about now? Do you have a girlfriend?"

I wish. "No."

"Are you gay?"

Shocked, he glared over his shoulder. "Hell, no!"

Heather struggled to keep a straight face at the pure outrage flashing in Royce's eyes. *Men*...and they thought women were overly sensitive! As if he were a cornered animal, his gaze shifted around the room, looking for an avenue of escape. Time to back off. For now it was enough that she'd learned another woman hadn't been the reason he'd broken things off with her. Hoping to put him at ease, she asked, "Can we at least be friends?"

He took forever answering. "We can try."

She sidled up to him, then ran a fingertip across the skin under his eyes. "You're tired. Hit the sack early tonight." She wished she could jump in bed with him and chase away the shadows darkening his eyes. Standing on tiptoe, she kissed his cheek. He pressed his hand to his face—whether to wipe away her touch or hold it closer, she wasn't sure.

"What was that for?" he grumbled.

"Friends sometimes kiss." She hesitated at the back door. "Where do you want the feed?"

"In the barn. Since Luke ordered it, he can unload it."

Grump. Heather waved, then left the house. She didn't have to peek over her shoulder to know Royce stood by the sink, watching her through the window. The heat of his stare burned her bare shoulders. Let him think they could be friends. She'd bide her time until he dropped his guard. Then she'd go in for the kill.

Chapter Seven

"You gonna hide in here all night?" Luke huffed from the doorway.

Royce lounged in his office chair, his legs resting across the top of his desk, a pile of mail sitting unopened in his lap. "And if I do…?"

Without being invited, the foreman hobbled into the room and sat down in the chair across from the desk. Bandit stretched out at his feet.

"There's a ham sandwich in the fridge if you're hungry."

"Thanks." After Royce had showered he'd passed on supper and gone straight to his office, determined to occupy his mind with something meaningful, like paying bills and sorting through his mayor-mail.

He was expecting a letter from the Atlanta State Park Board of Tourism. In February, he'd attended a meeting with park supervisors and proposed an advertising campaign to help increase tourism in the area.

But as soon as he'd sat down, his gaze had landed on Heather's high school graduation photo. He'd studied the picture, remembering that when she'd accepted her diploma he'd wondered what the future would hold for the ragtag hellion. Which tonight got him to thinking about *his* future—rather, the fact that he had no future…except the day-in and day-out monotonous life of a rancher and small-town mayor.

"I suppose you're pissed about the order Heather delivered from the feed store."

"Nope." Flipping through the envelopes in his lap, Royce pretended to show interest in one.

"What crawled inside your boots and bit you?" The old man grunted. "Can't fool me. You got feelin's for the girl."

"I don't want to talk about Heather, Luke."

"Watchin' you suffer in that hospital bed was the hardest thing I ever done." Luke gazed across the room in a trance, as if the past were replaying in front of his eyes. "The doc gave you enough morphine to knock a horse out, but you kept calling her name."

"Let it be."

As though sensing the tension between the two men, Bandit lifted his head and whined. Luke patted the animal's head. "Just tell me one thing."

The nosy fart wasn't going anywhere until he had his say. "Spit it out, then."

"Are you happy?"

"What kind of question is that?"

"The kind an old man asks when he's lived his whole life alone and don't want to see the young man he loves like a son suffer the same fate."

"What's done is done, Luke. Life goes on."

A sour expression puckered the foreman's face. "That's right. Life do go on, but the problem is, you ain't goin' with it."

Not in the mood to argue, Royce placed the mail on the

desk and stood. "I guess I am hungry. Think I'll head over to the Pine Top Café for a bite."

As mayor, he'd gotten into the habit of eating out twice a week to give the local citizens an opportunity to approach him with concerns or questions. He grabbed his Stetson off the hat rack by the door and strode from the room without another word.

Once the truck hit blacktop, he edged it over eighty. He'd driven this particular stretch of road so often he could navigate it blind. The possibility of a speeding ticket was next to nil. At six-thirty in the evening, everyone within twenty miles was eating supper at the café, including the sheriff and his two deputies.

As he sped around a sharp curve in the road, his heart skidded to a stop. Busted crates and chickens—live chickens—scattered across both lanes!

He slammed his foot on the brakes and clutched the steering wheel until the skin over his knuckles threatened to split open. Then he prayed like hell he wouldn't be eating poultry every night for the next two months.

When he jerked the wheel to the right to avoid squashing a hen, the tires hit a patch of gravel, sending the vehicle careening to the side of the road, where the truck came to a screeching halt less than a foot from the bumper of... *Heather's truck.*

Chest heaving, he sat immobile, the palms of his hands fused to the steering wheel. A drop of sweat trickled down his temple, and getting air into his lungs required major effort. About the time he heard the tap on the window, his pulse had dropped from the heart-attack zone to the anxiety-attack risk.

The door opened and a blast of humid air hit him in the face. "Are you all right?" Heather asked.

"Just tell me one thing," he growled, staring straight ahead.

"Okay."

"You're not having a poultry lottery, are you?"

Her soft laughter calmed his nerves and lowered his pulse rate to normal. Now that his emotions were under control, he looked Heather over from head to toe. Satisfied that she appeared uninjured, he released his death grip on the steering wheel and stepped from the truck. Spinning in a slow circle, he gasped. "Where did all the chickens come from?"

"Well, I thought it might be fun to dump a bunch of poultry in the road and watch cars swerve around them."

Sassy little thing. Her defiant blue eyes sparkled, lighting her whole face. Making her beautiful. Making him want her. Right now. Right here. Right in front of the damn chickens.

"Should I put these in the back of the truck?"

At the sound of a male voice, Royce glanced over his shoulder. A young man with a hen under each arm nodded a greeting. "Howdy, Mayor."

"Who the hell are you?"

"Westen James. Everyone calls me West."

Ah, Mr. Fast-hands from the Steer. Royce searched the road for a third vehicle. He spotted the truck parked up ahead on the opposite shoulder. "How did this happen, Heather?"

She shrugged. "The front tire blew. Then, when I hit the brakes, the crates in the back shifted and I lost control."

Royce moved to the front of the Ford and studied the damaged tire. Hell, the flat was in better shape than the three remaining bald ones.

"I don't have a spare," Heather said.

"Why doesn't that surprise me?"

The James kid joined them. "I offered to give her a lift out to my place to call a tow."

Royce glanced at the cell phone in Heather's hand. What a moron. He turned away to keep from busting up at the laughter in her eyes. Ignoring the idiot, he spoke to Heather. "My spare won't fit."

"Yeah, neither will mine." James set the hens in the back of Heather's truck. The birds fluffed their feathers and escaped over the opposite side.

Double moron. "Where do you live, James?"

The young kid settled a hand over his Texas-size belt buckle. "I'm working out at the Old Homestead Dude Ranch this summer."

"Listen up, East—"

"West. My name is West," he insisted, poking his puny chest out like a puffer fish.

"West. I'll handle things from here."

"But I—"

"So long, kid."

Red-faced, the cowboy spun away and grumbled something unintelligible all the way to his truck. He peeled onto the road, sending the fowl squawking toward the opposite side.

While Royce was contemplating the best way to secure the poultry in the back of his truck bed, Heather tapped his shoulder.

"I have a favor to ask."

What now?

"I need to get this order out to the Anders' place." She motioned to fencing wire in the truck bed.

"I thought I was your last delivery of the day."

"You were. But something came up."

"I suppose you left another sticky note on the door?"

She nodded.

Forget it. He wasn't about to go that route with her again. "Why are you hauling chickens around?"

"Mrs. Anders called the store and said Mr. Bunker was ill and couldn't deliver the chickens to her place. Since I had to go right past the Bunkers' to get to the Anders' ranch—"

Royce held up a hand, cutting her off. "So you're chauffeuring the Bunkers' chickens to the Anders."

"Mr. Bunker placed an order for over five hundred dollars' worth of fencing material from me two days ago." She gestured around her. "I didn't think it would be too much trouble to drive a few chickens down the road. Besides, Mr. Anders also wanted to enter the lottery."

He wondered what old men like Bunker and Anders wanted with a Mustang. The geezers were both nearing eighty. Jeez, Heather shows up and the whole town starts acting crazy.

"With Mr. Bunker's order I have enough money to pay the quarterly taxes. Any cash I bring in now will go toward back taxes."

Speechless, Royce stared at the chickens pecking the ground near his boots. *Well, I'll be damned.* The lottery idea had worked.

Good for her. Bad for him. Evidently, Nowhere was stuck with her for a while longer. "C'mon. Help me round up these fair-feathered friends of yours."

After twenty minutes, they'd recaptured the birds and stuffed them into the cages that hadn't busted apart. He loaded the poultry in his truck bed, while Heather collected the broken pieces of crate scattered every which way.

"Hop in. I'll drop you off at the store, then deliver the order."

"No."

"No?"

"I'm going with you. It's my delivery."

For the first time he noticed the paleness of her complexion. He wasn't the only one pushing himself too hard. The past couple of weeks he'd been thinking only of himself and the havoc Heather created in his life. Was it possible *his* behavior was putting Heather under the same kind of strain? "I'll deliver the chickens. You're going back to the store to rest."

"I'm not a child. I don't need a nap." Her lower lip trembled.

Instead of hugging her to him as he wanted to, he grabbed her elbow and escorted her to the front seat of his truck. Without thinking, he brushed a strand of loose hair behind her ear. "You're working too hard."

A tear dribbled down her cheek. "Stop bossing me around."

To heck with right or wrong. To heck with the consequences. For that matter, to heck with the whole frickin' world. He held her face, then rubbed the pad of his thumb over her bottom lip. His gaze never leaving her mouth, he lowered his head—

Abruptly a squealing siren blasted through the air, ending the almost-kiss. *Damn.* Royce stepped back just as the patrol car rounded the bend and pulled to a stop alongside the black Dodge. The officer rolled down his window.

"Evening, Deputy Harris. Heather could use a lift to the feed store."

After recounting the chicken story for the deputy, Royce held open the patrol-car door for Heather. Before she got in she whispered, "Who's going to rescue you next time, Royce?"

As he watched the police car disappear, he equated Heather to quicksand. Slowly but surely, she was sucking him under.

IT WAS BARELY SIX and already perspiration dotted Heather's brow as she buffed and rubbed the hood of the Mustang until the car shone.

She'd spent last night slumped in the front seat, listening to the radio and calling herself every kind of fool for sacrificing her beloved baby. But she'd made enough money with the lottery to keep the government off her back and the store open a little longer.

Regardless, she required an additional idea to boost sales to pay off the creditors. She hated to admit defeat, but maybe Royce was right. Perhaps she should sell. There was a small part of her that toyed with the idea of taking the easy way out.

But if she sold the business, she'd have no reason to stay in Nowhere. And right now, the last thing she wanted to do was leave. This...*something* between her and Royce demanded more exploring.

She tossed the rag into an empty bucket and went inside to shower. Fifteen minutes later, dressed in a white denim miniskirt and sleeveless print blouse, her waist-long hair caught up in a clip on top of her head, she cringed at her reflection in the mirror. Her skin's pasty hue made her look as if she were on her way to a funeral, not a lottery drawing.

Auctioning the car had been a sensible business decision. If she focused on that, she'd survive the morning without breaking down. The bell above the door jangled, bringing an end to the peace and quiet.

Clean-shaven and freshly showered, Royce stood at the front counter, holding his hat in one hand. "Sure you want to do this? There's time yet to call off the drawing."

She wouldn't let him see how much losing the car hurt. "I don't think the folks who bought supplies from the store would appreciate a cancellation." There was something disconcerting about the way he studied her. As if he were peeling the layers of her soul away, searching for the young girl he'd known years earlier—the same girl who'd instantly fallen in love with the used Mustang. He cleared his throat and put his hat back on.

"You're leaving?" She'd hoped he would stay and lend his support.

"I have work to do at the ranch."

How could he act as though this was just an ordinary day? "What if you win?"

He flashed a crooked smile. "You mean Luke, don't you?"

"Same difference." Shrugging, he walked toward the front door. "Good luck."

Fine. She didn't want him here if he didn't want to be here. After taking one deep breath, she straightened her spine, then went out back to face the mob gathering around the loading dock.

She milled through the crowd, smiling and waving. Convincing everyone that she was as excited about the drawing as they were. Even though she was losing the car, she admitted she was gaining something of more value in return.

Through purchasing supplies at the store, the citizens of Nowhere and the surrounding area had demonstrated their support and forgiveness of her hell-raising adolescent days. Many of them, in fact, showed more faith in her than her father ever had. To be accepted back into the fold after being gone so long humbled her and warmed her heart.

Heather stepped next to the Mustang and removed the large metal feed pail, filled with the lottery tickets, from the front seat of the car. She set the pail on top of an old crate.

Once the chatter and bursts of laughter dwindled, she smacked the side of the bucket with a dowel. "Before I pick the lucky ticket, I want to thank all of you for purchasing your supplies at Henderson's." Her throat tightened, making it difficult to keep a smile on her face. "I didn't know what to expect when I returned to Nowhere. Most of you remember me as…" She coughed. "Mischievous." Laughter rolled through the group. "And we all agree, my father wasn't a very nice man." The faces in front of her sobered. Swallowing hard, she trained her eyes on the back of the lot, hoping she wouldn't cry.

"I didn't expect such a warm welcome. Your support and friendship are more than I deserve." She took a deep breath, then forced herself to continue before she lost her courage. "I realize now how special this community is and I'm proud to be a part of it." She wiped the corner of her eye. "Without your support I wouldn't have been able to keep the store open."

She plunged her hand into the pail and swished the tickets around. Twice she grabbed one, then let the stub drop from her fingers.

With a surge of determination she selected the winning

number—*782*. Drawing on her last reserves of strength, she shouted the number into the crowd.

Everyone shuffled through their ticket stubs.

"Well, I'll be hog-tied. I got me the winnin' ticket." Amid cheering and groaning, Widower Higgins made his way to the front of the loading dock and held up his stub.

Heather gaped at the top of his shiny bald head. A seventy-one-year-old man with false teeth, blue overalls and mud-covered work boots had won her precious car. She accepted his ticket and compared the numbers, then she tugged the keys from her skirt pocket, and placed them in his gnarled hand. "Congratulations, Mr. Higgins."

"Thank ya, missy." He faced the crowd, then scowled at the young high school guys who had gathered around the car. "Git yer blasted paws off my new wheels." He shuffled over to the Mustang, slid into the front seat, turned the engine over and hollered, "Got me a date with the widow Murphy." The crowd guffawed and cheered as Mr. Higgins drove the car away at a snail's pace.

Heather was finding it difficult to breathe. Tears blinding her, she fled inside the store and locked the door behind her. She stumbled to her private quarters and fell onto the bed. Face smashed into the pillow, she cried. Deep, agonizing sobs. She'd given away a piece of her precious relationship with Royce. Given away one of the few good memories of growing up in this town. She wasn't aware how much time had passed by, when a large hand squeezed her shoulder. Gasping, she rolled over.

Royce stood next to the bed, hat in hand, a grave expression on his face. "I guess Luke didn't win the car."

New tears flooded her eyes and her heart twisted. Royce hadn't returned to the ranch. He'd come back.

Brushing the tears away with the back of her hand, she sniffled.

"Scoot over." He sat on the edge of the bed, then tossed the Stetson toward the chair in the corner. The hat landed on the seat. He held her hand, and the gentleness of the caress warmed and comforted her. Made her weak and vulnerable.

His dark gaze bored into her. "This is my fault."

"What?" she croaked.

"I shouldn't have let you get rid of the car."

She caressed his cheek, surprised when he allowed her touch. "The decision wasn't yours to make, Royce."

"But you regret losing it."

"I do. But it couldn't be helped."

He frowned, and she resisted the urge to trace the deep grooves across his forehead. "If I hadn't shown up on campus to tell you that your father died, would you have returned to Nowhere?"

She waited until he made eye contact with her. "No. Probably not."

Brown eyes held hers. "I felt it, too, that afternoon."

At his confession she sat up and inched closer to his side. "I thought I'd put you behind me, Royce. But then you waltzed into the day care, and it was as if all the hurt and anger over how you'd ended things with me came rushing back. I couldn't let you walk out of my life again without getting some answers."

"I'm not sure I'm ready to give you those answers."

"I'll wait until you are."

He gazed at her with such naked longing that Heather thought she'd die if he didn't want her. Seconds ticked by, but he made no move to touch her. She stroked his upper thigh and the hard-packed muscle bunched beneath her fingers.

Desire flashed across his face—along with denial. Why was he fighting this—them so strongly?

She leaned forward, hesitating when her breath mingled with his. Their bodies sizzled with desire, electrifying the air around them.

She licked her lips in anticipation. His quiet groan encouraged her. She danced her mouth across his, soothing the ache in her belly.

When she flicked the tip of her tongue against the corner of his mouth, he seized control of the kiss, forcing her lips apart, thrusting his tongue inside. This was the kiss she had yearned for…she remembered.

Feeling a little wild, a little out of control, she crawled onto his lap, straddling his thighs, pressing her breasts to his chest. His fingers dug into her hips, snuggling her closer until there was no mistaking his lust.

This time *she* groaned.

The skin along the inside of her legs tingled and quivered. Frustrated, she squirmed, then grasped his hands and brought them to her breasts.

He froze for one second before dumping her off his lap and onto the bed, where she landed in a heap. He confiscated his hat and backed toward the doorway.

KISSING HEATHER was like sucking a stick of dynamite. Her mouth was nothing short of explosive. She hadn't removed a stitch of clothing yet all hell had broken loose inside him. He longed so badly to give in, to give them both what they craved. But he feared that once he crossed the line with Heather, the damage to his heart would be irreparable.

There was an elemental level of honesty in her that awed him. She didn't mask her desire for him or make excuses for her feelings. The temptation to risk everything for a night in her arms was so real he could taste it.

Heather Henderson *touched* him. She was there, inside him all the time now. He yearned to make love to her, but he couldn't.

"This won't happen again. You have my word," he said.

His gut tightened at the sparks of passion still flashing in her sea-blue eyes. She popped off the bed, planted her feet on the floor and faced him defiantly. "What makes you so sure we won't get carried away the next time we're in a room together?"

His heart felt like a lead ball in the middle of his chest. "Because you're leaving on the next bus out of Nowhere."

Chapter Eight

"'Mornin', Fred." Royce greeted the barber as he entered the shop on Main Street across from Henderson Feed. He hoped he could get this meeting over with and return to the ranch before Heather even knew he'd been in town.

"Good thing you always carry that fancy cellular phone around with you. The three biddies in the back are chomping at the bit to talk to you."

Right now he cursed the wireless technology that had interrupted his morning. "What do they want?"

"Wouldn't say." Fred pointed out the front window. "Could you hurry it up? Those fellows won't come in until them uppity broads leave."

"I'll do my best." Royce passed through a doorway, followed a short hallway around a corner, then stepped into Fred's break room. Three woman in their fifties, if not older, sat at a Formica table, sipping coffee out of Styrofoam cups. They were dressed as if they'd just come from church, their leather handbags matching their shoes and antique heirloom jewelry glittering from their ears and throats.

"Ladies." He tipped his hat. "Royce McKinnon."

"Mr. McKinnon." The woman with iron-gray hair stood.

"I'm Thelma Crawford, president of the Payton County Preservation Society."

Great. The wife of the man Royce hoped to replace on the cattlemen's board. He offered a hand. "Pleased to meet you, ma'am."

"My associates, Victoria Brandt and Arlene Hilliard." The other two women remained seated and smiled politely.

He flashed his elect-me grin. "What can I do for you, ladies?"

The Crawford woman opened her designer purse and removed a white business envelope. "This is a letter informing you that a petition has been filed against a business in your town."

"What kind of petition?" His mind raced. Had he overlooked something in his mayor-mail the past couple of months?

"I'm sure you're aware, that..."

Great. A speech. He tapped his boot and pressed his lips together to keep from interrupting the woman's spiel.

"The Payton Preservation Society's purpose is to ensure all buildings with historical value in the county be preserved for future generations."

He'd run out of patience. "What building are you referring to?"

"Henderson Feed Store."

Heather's store had historical value?

"Six months ago we conducted a standard tour of all buildings in the county. We found Henderson's has been badly neglected over the years. If something isn't done soon, the building will be a total loss."

Now that the lady mentioned it, this past Thanksgiving

he remembered Melvin Henderson grumbling about a bunch of "fancy" women snooping around his store.

"What kind of historical value are we talking about?"

He couldn't recall her name, but the chubby one, who could double as an artillery tank, popped up from the table.

"The back portion of the building and the loading dock were constructed in 1900. The building and surrounding acres were first used as a feedlot for cattle being shipped north."

Obviously the lady had done her homework.

"In 1920, the building was converted to a mercantile when the lumber industry moved into the area. The front room was added, as well as additional storage. The mercantile went out of business twenty years later. In 1947, Mr. Henderson's father purchased the property and reopened the store. Upon his and his wife's deaths, the property reverted to their son, who..." The women exchanged exasperated looks. "Who let the building deteriorate to its current abhorrent condition."

"Are you ladies aware that Melvin Henderson passed away several weeks ago?"

"Yes, we're very sorry to hear that."

None of the women appeared a bit remorseful to Royce.

"We understand his daughter has returned to take ownership of the store."

"What do you want with the property?"

The tank sat and the head honcho stood. "We're requesting that you register the building with the Payton County Preservation Society and encourage Ms. Henderson to begin renovations immediately so we can save a piece of local history."

"Have you talked with Heather—I mean, Ms. Henderson—about this?"

"We have." Three sourpuss expressions stared back at him.

"What did Ms. Henderson say?"

"She wasn't interested in registering the building and isn't in a financial position to renovate the property."

"Well, then I guess you have your answer, ladies. I don't imagine there's anything else I can do for you."

"As mayor of Nowhere, you can serve this petition." Mrs. Crawford handed him the envelope.

He removed a letter and scanned its contents. After sifting through paragraphs of legal jargon, he understood the gist of the petition: fix the place up or prepare for a legal battle. Although Royce didn't take kindly to anyone coming into his town and bullying his merchants, he had to admit that this might be the break he was hoping for in convincing Heather to quit messing around with the store and finish earning her degree.

Mrs. Crawford nodded to the paper in his hand. "We'll return in a week to see if any of the improvements on the list have been completed."

One week? Were these women crazy or just plain mean-spirited?

"And if improvements aren't made?"

"Then our lawyer will be in touch with Ms. Henderson."

The trio filed out of the room.

What a mess. Royce didn't want to think about what Heather would say when he served her the petition. No way could she come up with the money to pay for all the renovations stated in the document in seven days. She'd have to sell.

Selling meant she'd return to College Station. Where she belonged. When all was said and done, he'd get his way and Heather would leave Nowhere. So why didn't that make him happy?

Conflicting emotions ate at Royce. On the one hand, he wanted Heather to leave so he could recapture a sense of peace and move forward with his life. On the other hand, he was getting used to having her create havoc in his daily routine. She might cause him extra worry and sleepless nights, but each morning as he stepped out of the shower a zing of anticipation shot through him when he contemplated what zany thing she'd do next.

He thought about the night at the Steer, when he'd followed her back to the store. He'd almost lost control and given in to his craving to make love to her. They were consenting adults, they had a history and they had feelings for each other. All he had to do was crook his finger and he was confident she would come running.

A hot and heavy summer fling was tempting. The only problem was that he couldn't have *just sex* with Heather. Nope. If they made love, his heart would become involved. He'd rather live the rest of his life wondering what it would feel like to make love to her than to live with the pain of never repeating the experience. Heather was young, full of energy, smart and had places to go. She deserved more out of life than he had to offer.

Royce left a brief message with his lawyer, asking the man if he would check over the petition, then he walked across the street to the feed store. No sense putting off the inevitable. Bad news wasn't like wine—it didn't get better with time. He entered through the front door, but Heather was nowhere in sight. He heard scuffling sounds and a muffled curse coming from the storage room.

The upper half of Heather's body disappeared inside an old pickle barrel, leaving her cute fanny sticking up in the air. Her cutoffs rode high on her thighs and he swore her underwear *should* have shown. Made him question whether she wore any panties at all. From where he stood in the doorway there wasn't even a tan line visible.

He shoved his hands into the front pockets of his jeans to keep from touching the firm swell of one buttock. "Want some help?"

"Noooooo!"

The muffled answer made him grin.

"What are you searching for in there?" He peered over the rim of the barrel, but her hair blocked the view of the bottom.

"My necklace."

The barrel threatened to tip. He steadied it with one hand, snuck an arm around her waist and lifted her out. Her head cracked against the side.

"Ouch!" She emerged red faced and breathless. With her long mop of hair covering her face and shoulders, she looked like Cousin It on *The Addams Family.*

"Let me turn the barrel over."

"Never mind, Prince Charming. I got the necklace." She opened her fist to reveal a silver chain with an oval locket. "If you're here to try to convince me to take the next bus—"

"No. This is official business." He pulled the petition from the back pocket of his jeans.

"Official business?" She eyed the envelope as if it might attack her. "Is that another tax bill?"

"The taxes are the least of your worries."

She held out her hand and he passed her the envelope. "I told those nosy women I wasn't interested in registering the store with the historical society."

"I put a call in to my lawyer to have him review it, but from what I can see, the petition looks legal, Heather."

"You mean if I refuse to repair the building, I'll lose it?" Her voice rose with each word.

"They're giving you one week to make progress."

"Well, how thoughtful." She tossed the petition into the pickle barrel and lifted her chin. "What happens if I do make the repairs?"

Was she crazy? Where did she presume she was going to get the money? "I'm not sure. I suppose they'll set a time frame for the repairs to be completed."

Her shoulders sagged. "Wonderful. Just wonderful."

He waited to feel a sense of relief at the sound of defeat in her voice, but the only thing humming through his body was frustration, because this was a jam he couldn't get her out of. "At least consider selling. Let someone else worry about updating the building."

"No one will want to buy the business if they know those old vultures go along with the deal."

She had a point.

"Fine. I'll…start with the roof. That ought to show the battle-axes."

"You can't afford a new roof."

"Oh, please. Shingles can't be that expensive."

"The petition states that you have to maintain the building's historical integrity."

"What does that mean?" She leaned over the barrel and retrieved the letter. Scanning the contents, she frowned. "It says here that because the town is surrounded by forest and gets a significant amount of moisture year-round, metal sheeting is recommended."

"Makes sense."

"Then why does the roof have regular asphalt shingles right now?"

"Because that's what your grandfather and father used. The building has at least three layers of rotting roof on it."

"Fine. I'll use metal roofing."

"Metal roofs are more expensive, Heather."

He hated watching the light fade from her pretty blue eyes. Before he could stop himself he offered, "Let me go over my finances. Maybe I can come up with the money."

The bell on the front door clanged. "Thank you, but no. I'll figure something out."

Stubborn woman.

HEATHER SAT on the edge of the bed, a pair of sturdy work boots on her feet, waiting to be laced up. Today was the Fourth of July. Last night, Amy had invited her to go with a group of friends to Houston and stay the night to watch the fireworks at the Space Center. If it hadn't been for the stupid petition, she would have closed the store an extra day and gone along.

Instead, she'd decided to celebrate the holiday by ripping off roof shingles. She glared at the boots, wishing she could use them to knock the Payton Preservation Society biddies upside the head.

Of all the sucky luck. Why had those women singled out Henderson Feed? Couldn't they have found another deteriorating building to claim? She thought about her father—something she tried to avoid most of the time. Had he known about the building's history? Not that he would have cared one way or the other. The only things the man had held dear were cigarettes, beer and his casino forays over the Louisiana border.

Shoving her father's memory aside, she concentrated on

the specifics of the petition. The letter had outlined several repairs and upgrades, the roof being at the top of the list.

She'd spent three days haggling with contractors, each agreeing to put a new roof on for little less than a fortune. After ten calls she found a man willing to charge her wholesale prices on the supplies if she removed the old roof and handled the cleanup herself.

Good thing she'd saved the birthday check Royce had given her in May. She hadn't wanted to touch the money—in case the store failed and she had to return to College Station, she'd need the cash to hold her over until she found a job. *Crud.*

She couldn't afford to sit around and feel sorry for herself. Besides, how hard could tearing off a bunch of roof shingles be? After consuming a granola bar and a can of Dr Pepper for breakfast, she confiscated a pitchfork from the storage room and prepared herself for a crash course in Roofing 101.

When she stepped out the back door, she almost fell on her face. Flats of metal sheeting and supplies sat stacked on the loading dock. The order she'd placed for the materials wasn't supposed to arrive until the day after tomorrow.

A piece of paper attached to one of the boxes fluttered in the breeze. Maneuvering around the supplies, she yanked the note loose. Tears burned the backs of her eyes as she read the message. Printed on official mayor stationery, the message stated that Henderson Feed Store was eligible for a grant from the town's newly established historical preservation fund. The grant received unanimous approval by town board members on July third.

Yesterday?

Plopping down on a pile of metal sheets, she stared around her in confusion. Royce wanted her to sell, but every time she had her back to the wall, he came to her rescue. Nothing about the man made sense.

"Looks like you could use some help."

Heather jumped. How long had Royce been standing in the shadows, studying her? She stood and brushed the seat of her shorts.

Dressed in a pair of ratty old jeans, a faded Dallas Cowboys T-shirt and scruffy work boots, he was the sexiest roofer she'd ever seen. "A historical preservation fund, huh?" She softened the skeptical tone in her voice with a smile.

He shrugged. "It was an economic decision. Keeping the store open means more people coming to town. More shoppers, more revenue for the other merchants."

Her smile widened to cover the pang of disappointment his explanation brought. For a fleeting moment, she'd hoped he had petitioned the city council members for *her*—because he'd changed his mind about wanting her to leave. "Are you here to work, or just talk?"

"Work. The others will be along shortly."

"Others?"

"I called in a few debts. Six, to be exact."

He may have purchased the supplies, but he wasn't running the show. "I'll let you and your debts help on one condition."

Laughter twinkled in his eyes. "You have a condition?"

Trying to keep a straight face, she insisted, "After the roof is replaced, you have to stay and watch the fireworks with me tonight."

He rubbed a hand along his jaw. "Does the invitation include supper?"

Leave it to a man to think about his stomach when a woman was thinking of…other things.

"I've got hot dogs."

"Enough for six men?"

"No."

"Drinks?"

"A six-pack of Dr Pepper."

Shaking his head, he fished his wallet from his back pocket and handed her three twenties. "Get enough hot dogs, sodas and chips for my crew and I'll watch the fireworks with you."

Her eyes narrowed. "I suppose I have to do all the cooking?"

He grinned. "Yep."

Nose in the air, she brushed past him. "Fine. I look forward to roasting all ya'lls weenies."

Chapter Nine

"I heard the mayor was pretty hard on you, too," Kenny Wilkinson muttered around a mouthful of hot dog. The exhausted sixteen-year-old sat with Heather on the loading dock at the end of the long day of roofing.

She'd been demoted to gofer after she'd accidentally kicked a fifty-pound pail of nails over the roof, missing Royce's head by mere inches. *Heather, grab the hammer, would you? Heather, toss more nails. Heather, hand me the water jug. Heather, move the ladder over a few feet.*

Kenny, along with six older high school students, had arrived mid morning. With Royce's guidance, the young men had toiled all day under the hot sun, tearing off old shingles and then slapping new ones down in their place. When they'd finished, Heather had finally been allowed to view the result. To her amazement, the roof looked as if professionals had done the job.

While Royce escaped inside the store to use her shower, she'd cooked four dozen hot dogs and the guys had inhaled most of them in record time. Approximately twenty minutes ago, they'd left to pick up dates for the firework display in Blairdsville later in the evening. Kenny had stayed behind, mumbling some excuse about checking his horse.

She figured the boy didn't have a girlfriend and had been too embarrassed to go stag with the others.

"Who told you Royce was hard on me?" She finished the last bite of her own hot dog.

"Luke."

"Well, he should know. He witnessed Royce and me go head to head a zillion times."

Instead of recognizing the humor in Heather's comment, Kenny expelled a long, drawn-out breath. "Luke says I should be grateful the mayor cares, but dang, he never cuts me any slack."

Heather wrapped an arm around his shoulders and offered a sympathetic squeeze. Embarrassed by the gesture, the teen blushed, and he edged sideways until her arm fell away.

Setting her can of cola next to her, she commented, "Funny thing about the mayor. The more he cares, the less slack he cuts you."

"You know what? I think he gets a kick out of making people miserable."

Smiling at the teen's grumpiness, Heather said, "There's a reason for making you miserable with all that work."

"Yeah, free labor in exchange for a few bales of hay."

"Royce is giving you something you can't understand yet, Kenny."

A frown creased the teen's forehead, but genuine interest shone in his eyes. "What do you mean?"

The faint squeak of a door hinge stopped Heather from answering immediately. Peeking over her shoulder, she scanned the back of the store but saw no one. "He's teaching you to take pride in your work."

Until her second year of college, Heather hadn't realized she'd even had a smidgen of pride. But when she'd almost failed biology, she'd dug her heels in and studied for the final until she'd gone cross-eyed. She'd made an A on the exam, and had done an extra-credit report, which had earned her a low B in the class.

"How's pride gonna help me?"

"Pride will get you through the rough times in your life and encourage you to make something of yourself."

The teen scoffed.

"I don't know what your home life is like, but my mom ran out on me and my dad when I was thirteen. I'm sure you've heard people talk about what a mean-spirited man my father was. If it hadn't been for Royce stepping in and watching over me, my life would be a real mess right now."

"My mom split six months ago."

Heather ached for Kenny. Almost a man, but still a boy, he yearned for a mother's love. "I'm sorry."

He shrugged. "Who needs her, anyway?"

You do, Kenny, more than you know. "I was pretty wild after my mom left. My dad stayed drunk most of the time. I got lonely, so to get attention, I acted up. Lucky for me, Royce pulled my butt from the fire before I could do too much damage to others or myself."

"I hate when the mayor asks if everything's okay. Like I'm gonna spill my guts and tell him 'No, everything ain't okay.'"

"When I was your age I kept most of my problems to myself. Now I wish I'd told Royce some of the things that happened."

"Like what?"

"Well, one time, I mentioned that the kitchen walls in the trailer were really dirty. Royce suggested painting them and I got all excited about the idea. The next day, I found a can of paint and a paintbrush on the trailer steps. While I was painting, my drunken father stumbled into the kitchen and fell against the wall, smearing the wet paint. He cursed me for hours for ruining his clothes. Instead of explaining to Royce what happened, I threw the paint supplies away and told him it had been a stupid idea."

"What did he say?"

"Nothing. He stared a long time at me—"

"Like he knew what you were thinking, right?"

Heather laughed. "Yeah, kind of like that. I had hurt his feelings, but instead of apologizing, I rebelled."

"How so?"

"I started skipping school. But that wasn't the worst of it. I got caught shoplifting once. And my senior year of high school I hung around with a bunch of losers. If not for Royce caring about me, I would have ended up in a juvenile detention center."

"If he's concerned, why does he act so tough all the time?"

"After a couple of years, I figured out his tough-as-nails lectures were his way of showing affection. Kenny, Royce's childhood wasn't all that great. His aunt and uncle were pretty old when he came to live with them after his parents died. I can't say for sure, but I doubt he received much affection from them, and because of that, he has a hard time expressing his feelings."

"Maybe. I just wish he'd let up once in a while."

"Stay out of trouble and keep your head on straight, and Royce will ease up." As much as Kenny grumbled about Royce's being a taskmaster, the boy had worked hard to please the mayor. And Royce had made sure the teen knew his help had been appreciated. He'd complimented Kenny and had encouraged him throughout the day.

Kenny peeked up at her. "Does he still get in your face now that you're older?"

"Yeah, sometimes. He wants what's best for me, but eventually, he'll have to trust that only I can determine that."

"I guess I could cut *him* some slack."

"Royce may be a pain in the backside, Kenny, but I wouldn't trade his yammering at me for anything. If not for him, I wouldn't have considered college. Wouldn't have even attempted to try to run this store on my own. His badgering gave me the confidence and courage to start believing in myself."

"My dad doesn't give a crap about any of us kids. If the mayor believes I might amount to something when I grow up, then maybe I will." Kenny checked his watch. "I gotta go."

Heather grabbed his arm before he could jump off the loading dock. "If you ever need someone to talk to…"

"Thanks." Red faced, the teen got in his truck and sped away.

"Where's Kenny going?" Royce stood by the back door.

Startled by his sudden appearance, Heather wondered if he'd eavesdropped on her and the teen's conversation. "Didn't say."

"I hope he stays out of trouble tonight."

"He's a good kid."

"Yeah. Bad family situation, but a decent young man."

"How was the shower?"

"Short." He chuckled.

"I imagine a man your size would have to bend a little to fit under the head."

"Bend? I got down on my knees."

"Now, that I would have liked to see—the mayor on his knees."

He patted his bare chest. "I thought I had an extra T-shirt in the truck, but I couldn't find the thing."

Heather's gaze took him in from head to foot. "I like your chest. I don't mind you going shirtless."

HELL, HE HATED when Heather spoke that way. Her flattery shoved him off balance. He crossed the loading dock in his flip-flops, carefully sidestepping the rusty nails littering the surface. "I told Kenny to clean this stuff up before he left."

"I'll sweep later." She stood, brushing her fanny off.

"Darn it, Heather. He has to learn—"

Her palm against his pectoral muscles trapped the next word in his throat.

"Kenny busted his butt for you today. He worked harder than any of the other guys. Ease up on the kid. Just because he doesn't finish one chore doesn't mean he'll serve time in the big house when he's older."

"But…" Her fingers walked a path down his chest, and he couldn't catch his breath.

"My, my, my." Her nail played with the hair that disappeared beneath the waistband of his shorts. "You have the kind of chest women dream about." When her index finger poked the inside of his belly button, he jumped.

"Powerful and deep." Her sigh made his skin shiver. "The kind of chest a woman could lay her head on at night and let the troubles of the day slip away."

"I could use that last beer in your fridge right now," he croaked.

Her eyes sparkled with humor. "Watch your dogs and I'll get it."

She knew she drove him nuts.

Standing by the small grill, Royce rolled each hot dog

over with his fingertip. He was tired, more tired than he'd been in a good while. But the day had been worth all the aches and pains he'd surely suffer tomorrow when he rolled out of bed. And amazingly enough, he'd spent an entire day with Heather and they hadn't argued. If circumstances were different, he and Heather would probably get along real well.

Grinning to himself, he decided he'd actually enjoyed today. The guys thought Heather was a lot of fun. He caught the teens trying to impress her with how fast they could pound a nail, or how many sheets of metal shingles they could carry up the ladder. Amazing how much work got done with a pretty woman around to show off for.

He supposed the fact that Heather had gone out of her way to compliment each of the boys on their brawn and brains had helped to boost their young egos. She'd smiled and had laughed at their silly jokes, making each of them feel special and appreciated. She really did have a way with kids—of all ages.

Heather would be a wonderful mother someday. Any child would be lucky to have her as their mother. For a fleeting moment, he pondered what it would be like to have a family with her. He pictured four kids—two red-headed girls and two blond boys, all with blue eyes.

"Last one." Returning with the lone beer, Heather handed the bottle over.

He unscrewed the cap and guzzled a long swallow before coming up for air.

"Taste good?"

She stared at his mouth, so he wiped his hand across his lips, figuring he must have drooled. He offered her a swig. "See for yourself."

"Being a good sport?" She winked, then stuck her tongue out and licked the rim of the bottle.

When she slid the tip of her tongue into the bottle opening, a groan rumbled in his throat.

"Hungry?" she asked.

Oh, yeah.

Gesturing to the blanket spread out on the loading dock, she added, "Have a seat." She doctored his hot dogs with relish and mustard, then piled potato chips on a plate and fetched a soft drink from the cooler.

"Aren't you eating the other one?" He nodded to the lone wiener still on the grill.

"I've had my fill. I'll sit and watch you eat." She pointed to the corner of his mouth. "Mustard."

Before he could use a napkin, she brushed the smear with her thumb. Her caress sent a spark racing through him.

They were silent for a few minutes while he finished his meal. Then he set his plate aside and asked, "Did you really mean it when you said you were glad I was so tough on you?"

"Eavesdropping is rude."

He grinned. "Answer me anyway."

She picked at her fingernails. "Yes, I'm grateful that you were always in my face while I was growing up. Still are, for that matter. You were a royal pain in the back end, but if not for all your meddling I'd probably have landed on the streets. Or gotten into drugs. Or worse."

A warm heat spread through him making him feel lethargic and mellow. And glad to be sitting with Heather on the loading dock. Until her confession, he hadn't realized how much he'd feared his interference in her life had been more detrimental than helpful.

"Why *didn't* you tell me your father had ruined the kitchen wall after you'd painted it?"

She shrugged. "I couldn't, Royce. I was afraid you'd decide I was too much trouble."

"Heck, girl, you couldn't have been any more bother than you already were." He softened the remark with a smile.

"Thanks a lot." She punched his arm affectionately. "Seriously. I didn't want you to make trouble for my dad, because he'd threatened to move away when you'd confronted him about being a better father. I couldn't stand the thought of never seeing you again."

The tears shimmering in her eyes made his gut tighten. "I would never have let him take you away, Heather." He tugged her close to his side. Right then he didn't give a flip that he wasn't wearing a shirt or that someone might drive into the alley behind the store and see them. All he cared about was holding her and chasing her bad memories away.

She pressed her lips to the base of his neck. He swore he heard her purr. A little longer—he'd hold her a little longer, then set her free.

"You're really a softie underneath all that grouchiness, aren't you."

He cleared his throat. "You were right when you told Kenny I didn't grow up with a lot of affection."

She traced his collarbone with the tip of one fingernail and his skin broke out in bumps. "I'm sorry, I shouldn't have said anything."

"Hush." He guided her head down to his shoulder, enjoying the feel of her in his arms. "My aunt and uncle didn't want me. But they were too embarrassed to admit it publicly, so they took me in. After a while I realized, no matter how well I behaved or acted I wasn't going to get a hug from either one of them or a kind word. I worked hard at my chores and in school, but nothing made a difference in how they treated me."

Heather's arms came around his waist and he drew comfort from her gentle squeeze.

"That's why you care so much about Kenny? You see yourself in him?"

"I suppose. But I don't always know the right things to say to him."

"Don't worry. The boy respects you, Royce."

"I wouldn't go so far as saying he respects me. But I do hope after his talk with you today that he believes I care about him."

"He believes."

"What about you, Heather? Do you believe I still care about you?" He gazed into her eyes, thinking they were almost big enough to swallow him up.

"Yes. I'd even go as far as saying that I believe you feel more for me than plain old caring, but you're too chicken to admit it."

You have no idea how close to the truth you are, babe. Before the conversation headed in a direction he didn't want it to go he asked, "Were you serious about climbing on the roof and watching the fireworks?"

"Yep."

Glad she'd allowed him to change the subject, he added, "Blairdsville is the closest town setting off fireworks tonight. That's twenty miles west of here. I doubt we'll see anything this far away."

"I know. We'll have to pretend."

He shook his head. "Let me get this straight. You want to climb up on the roof and *pretend* to watch the fireworks?"

"You game?"

"You're crazier than I thought."

She planted a smacking kiss on his lips. "C'mon. Live a little."

"CAN'T SAY MUCH for the fireworks, but the stargazing isn't bad," Royce commented, staring heavenward into the night sky.

Heather jabbed her elbow playfully in his side. Stretched out on a blanket at the far end of the roof, they'd been watching the sky for over an hour without catching a single flash of color. Not that she expected to see any. "I love that smell."

"Maybe I'll switch my deodorant bar to the tropical rain-forest soap in your shower."

"You nut." She sniffed loudly. "Rain. I smell rain coming." She rolled to her side and nudged his shoulder. "Mmm. Your tropical rain-forest-scented body makes me think of Tarzan and jungles."

"This Tarzan is beat. If you'd stop gabbing I could catch a nap up here."

She giggled. "I like talking with you. It's a nice change from arguing."

"Fine. What do you want to talk about next?"

"Government. What's your least favorite thing about being the mayor?" She suspected being mayor of Nowhere was more important to Royce than he let on.

"That came out of left field."

"The ranch is a lot of work. Then you add all the interruptions, phone calls and meetings…" She shrugged. "Just wondered if all that responsibility didn't feel overwhelming."

"Generally, I don't mind the interruptions. Besides, as

mayor I get to drive your Mustang in the Blairdsville parade every year."

She leaned up on her elbow. "You drive my car in the parade?"

He tugged her braid. "Yep, every year. Gives me an excuse to tune up the motor and make sure she purrs pretty for the crowd."

"How come you never *asked* me if you could drive the car?"

"Because I didn't think you'd mind."

"Hmm." She minded, but it seemed like a silly thing to argue over. After all he was storing her car free. "When your term is up, will you run for office again?"

Royce crossed his arms behind his head. "I've been tossing around the idea of running for the State of Texas Cattlemen's Association Board of Directors."

"Wow. That's a mouthful. Sounds important."

"One of the directors of the board plans to retire this fall. He's agreed to endorse me if I decide to run," Royce explained, intentionally leaving out the fact that the man's wife was the woman spearheading the movement to gain possession of Henderson Feed. "I'd like to run, but it's not that simple."

"How so?"

"For one, I don't have a college degree." Royce sat up and wrapped his arms around his bent knees.

"Do you need a degree?"

"No, but the other board members have them." He angled toward her.

"Degree or not, that man wouldn't offer to endorse you if he didn't believe you were qualified for the job."

The moon and stars provided enough light for Heather

to catch the dark shadow that fell across his eyes. He'd always seemed so secure; to realize he might not have the confidence to run for a seat on the cattlemen's board was a bit disconcerting. At least now she better understood why he was adamant she earn her degree.

She touched his cheek, needing to console him, to offer some kind of comfort. "Have you thought about taking correspondence courses?"

He nodded, his whiskers tickling her palm. "I've accumulated eighteen credits over the past two years. But I have a long way to go before completing the requirements for a business degree." He shifted from her touch as if uncomfortable with her sympathy. "You'd better get a move on it, or I'll have my degree before you."

"Funny, funny." She searched for the Big Dipper in the sky while considering how her relationship with Royce had evolved.

Those first turbulent years after her mother left, she'd had a love-hate relationship with him. One day she was thankful he was in her life; the next she'd wished he would bug off. When she'd gone off to college, she'd missed him dreadfully. But after the first year, she'd stayed busy with her friends and classes. Once in a while, he'd stuck his nose into her business, but generally, he left her alone.

Then that had all changed the April afternoon he'd stopped at her apartment angry and upset that the university had forwarded to him a letter containing information about her having switched majors again. She remembered her reaction to seeing him after three long years.

How handsome she'd thought he was—still was, for that matter. She'd noticed him in a purely sexual way. Before she'd even gotten over the shock of her physical reaction to him, he'd started lecturing. Tempers had flared and then she'd done something incredible—she'd kissed him. Right on the mouth.

She'd only thought to shut him up so she could explain, but before she'd stepped away, his mouth had opened over hers and he'd slid his tongue inside, and oh…man. Like a felled giant redwood, she'd fallen hard. Royce's one kiss had made her feel things she'd never experienced with any of the guys she'd dated in school.

Pretty soon, that one kiss turned into two, then three. Then she'd lost count. She'd been on the verge of collapsing against him when he'd finally torn his mouth from hers.

Never had anything so arousing, so exciting happened in her life. When it was over, she'd been sure the stunned look on his face had matched hers. He'd remained silent, his fingers stroking her skin, her hair, and she'd sensed that he'd been waiting for her to decide if what they'd done was right or wrong.

Right. What they'd shared had definitely been right.

When he'd finally left her apartment a few minutes later, she'd believed in her heart that what they'd shared had been special and more than just a kiss. He'd asked her to think about coming home for the summer and promised to call her, then had driven away. Days had turned into weeks. Near the end of May, she'd phoned him. It was over before it had even begun.

He tapped her forehead. "What's going on in there?"

"I was thinking about the past…the first time we kissed."

His body stiffened, then he exhaled loudly. She expected him to call an end to the evening, but he surprised her by remaining seated. She sensed the struggle waging inside him. Fearing he'd lose the battle with himself and turn away, she curled an arm through his, then laid her cheek on his shoulder.

"I thought that day was the start of something new and good between us."

As if her statement had caused him pain, he winced. "I thought so, too."

"What went wrong, Royce?" When he didn't answer, she asked, "Was it me? Did you regret kissing me?"

"Hell, no."

The fierceness in his voice convinced her that he spoke the truth. Seeming agitated, he lay down and snuggled her to his side. "What we shared…our kiss…I've never talked about with anyone. Not even Luke."

"Royce, you don't have to—"

"Yes, I do. You deserve to know why I didn't call. Why I broke things off with you."

She burrowed against him, prepared to wait forever if that was how long it took for him to explain.

"I'd planned to phone you the minute I got back to Nowhere. But I came upon a stranded motorist a few miles from the ranch. I called Luke on my cell phone to tell him someone needed help and I'd be a few minutes late."

His chest rose, then shuddered under Heather's head. Instinctively, she sensed the story of the stranded motorist was not going to have a happy ending.

"When I asked the woman what was wrong with the car she said she wasn't sure. My head was still crowded with thoughts of you, or I might have paid more attention. Instead of getting in the car and trying to start it, I stuck my head under the hood and checked the motor."

He squeezed her hand and she braced herself, not sure she wanted to hear the rest of the story.

His voice dropped to a whisper. "They came up behind me. Must have been hiding in the ditch on the opposite side of the road."

Royce's heart pounded beneath her ear, and she hated that after three years the memories still upset him deeply.

"Two guys grabbed my arms and another one used my gut for a punching bag. The woman took my wallet from my pocket and the cell phone from the clip on my belt. She flung the phone into the brush across the road. Then she dug her hands into my front pockets and grabbed my truck keys. They had my wallet and keys, so I figured they'd just take off."

There was more?

"One of the guys got a baseball bat from the car and told me to turn around and put my hands behind my head."

"Oh my God, Royce." Tears blurred Heather's vision and she clung to him, wishing with all her might she could erase the past.

"I braced myself for the blow, praying they wouldn't break my back."

Tears leaked from the corners of her eyes. Never would she have imagined something so horrible had happened to Royce.

"The pain was like nothing I'd ever felt in my entire life. I fell to the ground, thinking I was going to die. I couldn't breathe, couldn't move. I must have fallen unconscious. The next time I woke up I was in the hospital and Luke was at my bedside."

"I can't imagine how terrifying that must have been. They could have killed you, Royce!" She hugged him tightly. "Did the police ever catch the thugs?"

"No. An El Paso sheriff found the truck stripped down south of the city."

She hugged him even closer. "I'm just so thankful they didn't hurt you any worse. It's amazing you aren't still suffering any back pain."

"They didn't hit my back, Heather."

"Then…"

"They hit me…between the legs." He looked at her, his eyes filled with pain.

Oh, God. Tears spilled down her face. "You mean you can't…"

"If you're asking whether I can still perform the answer is yes. But when the doctor was surgically repairing the damage to my testes, he discovered something else."

His jaw clenched and Heather feared the worst. *Was Royce talking cancer?* "What did they find?"

"The correct medical term is *congenital bilateral absence of vas deferens.*"

"Meaning…?"

"I'm sterile."

Chapter Ten

Sterile?

Royce didn't deserve this.

The shuttered look in his eyes convinced Heather that he wouldn't reach out to her. He stood, then moved several feet away. He seemed so aloof. So cold. So detached from what he'd just revealed.

She wished he'd pull her close. Wished he'd do or say something besides stand there frozen. Tears blurred her vision. How often had she dreamed of them having their own family? Of little Royces and little Heathers running loose around the house while two harried parents chased after them?

She attempted to speak, but her aching throat trapped the words inside her. Then she did the most stupid thing. She burst into tears.

"Ah, baby. Don't." He moved quickly, gathering her up in his arms and tucking her head beneath his chin. She bawled like a ninny. Bawled for him. For her. For them.

When he brushed his mouth against her temple, she cried even harder, knowing that *she* should be comforting *him*. "It doesn't matter. It doesn't matter," she sobbed against his warm skin.

"Yes, Heather it does." Strong fingers bit into her arms and pushed her back.

"No…no." She reached for him, but her fingers brushed air. "I swear it doesn't matter to me, Royce. I'm just so thankful that it wasn't something more serious." *Like cancer.* She shuddered, unable to envision Royce not being a part of her life anymore.

"Of course it matters. I can't give you a baby, Heather."

"I don't need children to be happy." The thought of not holding her own child in her arms saddened Heather—but the thought of losing Royce was a pain she couldn't live with.

His face taut with strain, he cursed. "Right now you may believe you don't want children. But what if you change your mind?" He shook his head. "You deserve to have your own family someday."

At least now she understood the reason he kept pushing her away. The reason he hadn't called her all those years ago. An almost fierce protectiveness welled up inside her. Lord, how she loved this man.

"There's no sense starting a relationship that has nowhere to go, Heather."

She grasped his hand, then pressed his palm to her heart. "Just because you can't give me a child doesn't mean what I feel for you in here will go away."

The anger and frustration drained from his face. He held her to him and rubbed his cheek against hers in a tender caress. "Right now you might believe you can live without kids, but—"

Heather shushed him. "Don't give up on us before we even have a chance to be."

"You're asking the impossible from me."

Heather held his head between her hands and stared

him straight in the eye. "Think about it. Think about *us*. Just please don't say no, yet."

"Ah, Heather. What am I going to do with you?"

ROYCE WANTED Heather. In a bad way.

The band kicked up another tune, and his gut tightened another notch as he watched another young cowboy twirl Heather around the hay-strewn barn floor at the Eight of Spades Ranch outside Blairdsville. Royce had been hoping Heather wouldn't show up at the annual summer barbecue put on by the Cantrell family.

The slim-fitting, green dress hugged Heather's curves and squeezed her breasts until the smooth, plump mounds peeked above the low-cut bodice. The white cowboy boots made her legs appear long and sleek, sparking his imagination with wild images of her boots tangling with his on a nice comfy bed. Silver combs secured the messy mop of golden-blond hair atop her head. Several strands tumbled around her shoulders in a tousled mess, making him think she'd been fooling around in the hayloft. She passed within ten feet of him, and he swore he caught a whiff of honeysuckle perfume amid the tangy smells of barbecue beef and roasted corn-on-the-cob.

Royce still didn't have a clue what to do with Heather. As she'd promised, she'd given him time to consider their relationship—to come to terms with what she wanted—what she was willing to settle for. In truth, her reaction had shaken him deeply. He'd figured once she'd discovered the truth she'd accept that anything serious or permanent between them was impossible. He admitted that he'd gotten choked up at her fierce insistence their relationship continue full speed ahead.

Everything inside him yearned to take what she offered. But he had a feeling sleeping with Heather, then watching her walk out of his life would be more painful than the bat he took between the legs.

"Heather the hellion grew up right pretty, didn't she."

"Howdy, Mitch." Royce offered a hand to the owner of the Eight of Spades Ranch. "Another great turnout."

"Beth's doing. She loves planning this shindig every year." The two men eyed the dancing couples on the floor. "I heard Heather was running the feed store. How are things going?"

Royce's chest tightened with pride and a bit of worry. "Better than I'd anticipated." He'd been positive she'd give up after the first week or two. Her strength and determination had surprised him, and secretly pleased him.

"I hope you're still considering the open seat on the cattlemen's board. You'd do a fine job representing this area of Texas."

"I haven't ruled out running for the position," he answered, never taking his gaze off Heather. Her beauty, grace and youthful zest mesmerized him. The younger man twirling her around the floor made Royce wish he could turn back time.

Luke ambled over and joined the discussion. The foreman brought up the subject of beef prices and he and Mitch got into a heated debate. "If we don't have a good hay crop we'll have to sell early again this year."

"I'm using a new pesticide on the market. Should keep the beetles under control." Mitch set his beer bottle on a hay bale behind him. A group of rambunctious boys ran by and knocked the hay, spilling beer onto Mitch's polished boots. The rancher chuckled and grinned fondly at the ruffians.

Luke snapped his suspenders. "We can't hold out too long before goin' to market. The dang price for feedlot beef has dropped two months in a row."

Royce listened halfheartedly, more interested in keeping track of Heather on the dance floor.

"What do you think, Royce?"

Startled by Mitch's question, he grumbled, "Sorry. I didn't catch that."

Both Mitch and Luke grinned. "Go ask her to dance," Luke urged, nudging Royce with an elbow.

Mitch motioned with his beer to a woman dancing next to Heather. "Rebecca Hasley's only a year or two older than you, Royce. She's got a nice-size spread over in Green Valley. From what I hear, that no-good ex of hers already remarried."

Royce ignored the silly-ass grin on Luke's face. The foreman knew darn well he hadn't been eyeing Rebecca Hasley. His eyeballs had been glued to Heather.

Patting Royce's back, Mitch encouraged him. "About time you settled down, found yourself a wife, had a few kids and ran for the board." He strode off to greet another group of guests.

"He's right. That divorcee's got a nice spread." Luke moved his cud from one cheek to the other, then lowered his voice. "She already has two boys of her own."

His gaze narrowed on Rebecca. Brunette, small-boned and slim, she was an attractive woman. She was also subdued, calm, very businesslike—the exact opposite of Heather. And he'd met her boys a year ago. They seemed like good kids. She wouldn't mind that he couldn't give her more children.

But he didn't want Rebecca. He wanted Heather.

Suddenly, he wasn't in the mood to talk politics, beef or Rebecca. "Later, Luke." He wove through the dancers on the floor and tapped the shoulder of the redneck who had both arms around Heather's waist. "I'm cutting in."

The guy took one look at Royce's expression and headed for the beer kegs near the buffet tables.

"I thought you'd never ask me to dance." She smiled, eyes sparkling.

Those blue orbs entranced him. He doubted she realized how they revealed her moods and emotions—glowing when she was happy, losing their luster when she was sad.

Deciding to take her lead and act as if nothing had changed between them, he stepped closer and wrapped an arm around her waist, then moved to the music. "Hard to grab a dance when every guy in the place wants your attention." He spotted his foreman watching them. Ignoring Luke, he whirled Heather to the other end of the dance floor.

She inched closer and rested her forehead against his shoulder. She wasn't acting the way he'd expected a woman to act when she discovered the man she was attracted to couldn't father any children.

Someone bumped her from behind, and she moved closer still. Instead of putting some space between them, he pressed his palm to her lower back until he could feel her aroused nipples poke against his chest. Need rocked him back on his boot heels.

He could deny they had a future together all he wanted, but nothing would change the fact that he hungered to make love to Heather. He wanted to know how it would feel to hold her all through the night and wake up with her by his side. He wanted to create new memories to help him through the next fifty years.

The fast-paced two-step faded into a slow waltz. "One more dance." He couldn't make himself let her go.

"Sure."

The sultry answer reminded him of smooth suede and aged whiskey.

Her soft hair tickled his chin, and he fought against the urge to bury his face in the tangled mass. Perfume mixed with the subtle scent of her body floated around him. The seductive sway of her hips threatened his sanity.

Then she purposefully brushed her pelvis against his arousal. Before he did something to embarrass them both, he grabbed her wrist, led her across the dance floor and out a side door into the dark, humid evening.

As soon as the door closed and he was alone with her he gave in to his passion for her. He pressed her up against the side of the barn and thrust a thigh between her legs. He couldn't see her expression in the dark, but tiny, quivering puffs of air hit his neck, convincing him that she didn't object to his brash behavior. Her fingertips dug into his upper arms and the heel of her boot scraped the back of his calf. He ground his thigh against her, wringing a whimper from her.

He tilted her chin, until their mouths barely touched. His breath mingling with hers, her moan vibrated against his lips. *She wants me. I want her. Nothing else matters.* He thrust his tongue inside her mouth, where he lost himself in her taste. *Pure heaven.*

He didn't know how they got there, but suddenly, his hands lifted her breasts…massaging the soft mounds, caressing the swollen flesh, flicking the hard little nubs.

Somewhere in the distance a dog barked, bringing him to his senses like the whack of a two-by-four across his back. He shoved away from her, almost stumbling over a rock behind his boot. He whipped his hat off and tunneled his fingers through his hair, then stomped several feet away and gazed unseeingly at the night sky.

What in the hell was he doing?

"Royce?" Her voice trembled—from passion or anxiety, he wasn't sure.

Hands fisted at his sides, he faced her. "I'm sorry, Heather. I shouldn't have let things go that far."

"But—"

"I forced you—"

"Forced me? What are you talking about?"

He leveled a hard look at her, but she refused to back down. The sassy wench was going to make him say it. Lay it out in the open, word for word. "I thought maybe you might have changed your mind about us and having…sex." He hated admitting his insecurity, but Heather had a way of making him toss his pride aside.

"You think I've changed my mind? I think *you're* the one who's not sure."

"Exactly when did I say I didn't want to have sex with you?"

He hoped like hell there weren't spectators hiding in the bushes.

She shoved away from the barn and walked toward him. Placing her palm on his heart, she whispered, "It doesn't matter to me, Royce, that you can't father children. That isn't the reason I want to be with you."

"You say that now, but—"

"Royce. This is about trust. You trusting me."

She was right. So how could something so simple, like trust, be so difficult for him?

"Just so it's clear, I'll say it straight out. I want to make love with you. I want to sleep with you. I want to have sex with you. I want to be intimate with you. And last, I want to see if there's a future for us."

"Heather…I—we… Are you sure you want to take things between us further?"

"What's the matter, Royce?" she purred against his neck. "Afraid you might discover you can't live without me?"

That's it. He bent to scoop her up in his arms and carry her to his truck, but froze when the envelope in his back pocket fell to the ground.

"What's that?" She stepped out of the way so he could retrieve the envelope.

Blast! He'd forgotten all about the letter. Heather could make a sane man insane. A wise man a fool. "Arrived in the mail today. It concerns the store."

"Have the old biddies from the preservation society struck again?"

"'Fraid so. I don't think they expected you to take them seriously and begin making repairs."

"So?"

"So now they're demanding you fix the electrical and plumbing, which, by the way, isn't up to code."

"What if I can't afford to?"

"Then they'll pursue legal means to shut you down."

"We'll just see about that."

"Heather, how are you going to come up with the money? Put the store up for sale and be done with it once and for all."

The main reason Heather had returned to Nowhere to run the feed store was Royce. Now that she had the answers she'd sought, she wanted him to say something, anything that might give her an indication that he wanted her to stay. His silence on that front told her she had more work to do before he'd believe that they belonged together—forever.

Royce made her complete. Made her whole. Giving up the store meant giving up on her and Royce and their future. "I'm not ready to sell."

HE SHOULDN'T BE HERE.

Not this late at night.

The considerate thing to do would be to wait until morning to give Heather the bad news. But three days had passed since the barbecue at the Eight of Spades Ranch and he couldn't stay away from Heather any longer.

Royce sat in his truck behind the feed store and debated going inside. He wished like hell she didn't always make him lose his footing around her. After tossing in bed for two hours, he'd thrown on some clothes and headed for town.

He blamed this middle-of-the-night visit on her phone call at suppertime. She'd informed him that she'd secured a bank loan to pay for the store's electrical and plumbing upgrades. The woman was just full of surprises. Surprises he applauded. Even admired. But hated just the same. Heather was proving she could stand on her own two feet—without his help.

And that was the problem. He wanted her to need him. He wanted to solve her problems. To offer her advice. In his simple, guy brain it all boiled down to one thing: he couldn't give Heather children, so he needed her to need him in other ways. He hated this feeling of insecurity.

This unmanly need for reassurance was the reason he sat outside the store in the middle of the night.

If he was smart, he'd turn the truck around and haul his

sorry butt back to the ranch before anyone got wind of this insane, late-night visit. Too bad his brain had taken a vacation after Heather had blown into town. As long as he was here, he might as well go inside and check on her.

After removing a spare key from the glove compartment, he left the truck. The bright fluorescent lights blinded him when he stepped inside the storage room. Music that sounded suspiciously like jazz drifted through the store. What in the world was she doing up at this ungodly hour?

"Heather? It's me, Royce."

He found her slumped on a stool behind the counter, rubbing her eyes. The sight of her grumpy face brought back memories of the night he'd caught her trying to hitch a ride with a Florida trucker on the evening of her fifteenth birthday.

He'd spent the rest of the night sitting in a lawn chair outside the trailer, trying to convince her that running away wouldn't make her life easier. By the time he'd gotten her to promise to stay in school and not leave, that bastard father of hers still hadn't returned home. Royce had slept in his truck that night, then given her a ride to school the next day.

This time, however, she wasn't fifteen. She was twenty-five. And instead of tucking her in for the night and leaving, he wanted to get in bed with her and stay there.

"What are you doing here, Royce?"

Tenderness filled him at the sight of sleep creases along her cheek. Her loose hair fell down her back in tangles and he shoved his hands into his pockets to keep from brushing the strands out of her eyes.

"I realize I shouldn't be here this late—"

Waving a hand through the air, she cut him off. "Has something happened?"

"The phone rang. By the time I answered, whoever had called hung up. I thought it might have been you," he lied.

A corner of her mouth twitched, and he had a feeling she didn't believe his half-baked explanation. Embarrassed, he motioned to the laptop computer, piles of papers and stacks of books. "What's all this?"

Her eyes widened, then she gathered everything into one big, messy heap. "Stuff." She closed the laptop.

"Stuff?"

"Oh, all right." She scowled, searching through the clutter. "Here."

He took the sheet of paper she held out but couldn't make heads or tails of the columns and numbers across the page.

"You ruined my surprise." Her eyes shot little sparks.

"What surprise?" He handed the paper back, thinking how cute she looked when she was in a snit.

"I'm earning that infamous degree you seem to believe I'll never get."

"You're writing a paper?"

"Yep. Two, as a matter of fact. In light of my father's death, the professors made an exception and agreed to let me complete my classes by correspondence."

She didn't quit on me. He cleared the hoarseness from his throat. "I'm impressed."

"Thanks."

An awkward silence ensued as waves of heat, the kind a meteorologist couldn't predict, shimmered between them. When she didn't make the first move, he said, "I guess I'd better go."

Flashing a naughty grin, she asked, "Don't I get a congratulatory kiss?" She hopped off the stool and moved in front of him. Her flaxen hair caught the light and shined. Her mouth went soft, opened slightly and tempted him beyond reason.

"I didn't come here looking for this."

"Really? I'm disappointed."

He almost laughed at the cute way she pursed her lips.

"Then why did you come, Royce?"

"Because you haven't returned Mrs. Crawford's phone calls."

"I refuse to talk to that mean old lady." Heather leaned closer, her breasts tantalizing and teasing. "So what does the witch want with me this time?"

He shifted his hips, wondering if she'd felt his arousal. "She called about a meeting this Thursday."

Her lips feathered over his jaw. "A meeting…?"

He felt dizzy, then he remembered he'd been holding his breath and gulped a lungful of air. "You have to be there."

"Why?"

Was that her tongue he just felt in his ear? "Ahh…because."

"Because why?"

"Because you're being sued."

Chapter Eleven

Sued?

Ridiculous.

Absurd!

Late Thursday afternoon, Heather paced outside the Blairdsville Chamber of Commerce building, waiting for Royce and his lawyer. Minutes earlier, Thelma Crawford and the lawyer for the Payton County Preservation Society had leveled identical cool glances at her as they'd entered the building. Mrs. Crawford seemed to have it out for her, and Heather wished she knew why the building meant so much to the old toot.

Heather admitted she might be in over her head with the store, but concentrating on business affairs was the last thing on her mind right now. Aside from being preoccupied with researching her term papers, she was still reeling from the shock of finally learning the real reason Royce had ended their relationship three years ago.

She'd done a lot of crying over the past couple of weeks. She had cried for Royce. For the fear he must have felt when those thugs had attacked him. For the physical pain he'd endured. Images of him lying alone in a hospital bed had made her weep even harder. She'd cried for his foolish pride that wouldn't allow him to need her. Cried for the emotional pain he still suffered because of his sterility.

If anything that traumatic ever happened to Heather, she knew she couldn't survive without him by her side. As much as they'd gone head to head over the years, there wasn't any person on earth that she trusted more than him.

In the grand scheme of life, his sterility was a not-so-big deal. One way or another, she had to convince Royce he was still worthy of her love.

"Heather?"

At the sound of her name, she turned, then barely managed to keep her mouth from dropping to the sidewalk. Royce stood there hatless, his rich, rust-colored hair gleaming in the sun. Wearing a charcoal suit, white shirt and maroon tie, he reminded her of a wealthy oil baron, not a rancher.

Gracious, he was a handsome man.

He appeared cool and fresh in the sweltering July heat, while she felt frumpy and hot in her khaki skirt and sleeveless, black cotton sweater.

Royce motioned to the gentleman at his side. "Heather, this is Harold Mason. Harold, I'd like you to meet Heather Henderson."

The small, wiry man shoved a bony hand in her direction. "How do you do, Ms. Henderson."

Her stomach pitched. As far as first impressions went, the lawyer left a lot to be desired. His slight build and Coke-bottle glasses made her think he'd spent his childhood dodging bullies. This man wouldn't stand a chance against the high-powered lawyer the preservation society had hired.

Hiding her disappointment, she shook his hand. "Hello.

Thank you for coming." She glanced at Royce. "They're already here."

"Then we'd better go inside." He motioned for Heather to lead the way.

Inside the building, they walked down the main hall to the last door on the right. The lawyer entered the room first, and she would have followed if Royce hadn't snagged her arm. "Give Mason a chance, Heather. He may not look as slick as those bigwig city lawyers, but he knows his stuff. Trust me."

The apprehension knotting her insides eased at the conviction in Royce's voice. She nodded, then stepped into the lion's den.

A large mahogany table graced the center of the conference room. The blinds on the far wall were flipped to block the late-afternoon sun, but a few rays filtered through, spotlighting the dancing dust particles in the air.

As she approached the table, her sandals sank into the plush carpet. Mrs. Crawford and her lawyer were seated on the far side of the table. He wore his hundred-dollar haircut and thousand-dollar suit like a coat of armor. His beady eyes and narrow nose reminded her of a hawk. When his steady gaze settled on her, she felt like a tiny field mouse about to become his next meal. Standing, he offered his hand.

"Ms. Henderson, I'm Donald Weber. I'll be representing the Payton County Preservation Society as well as Mrs. Crawford's interests."

Much too smooth and self-assured for her taste, she disliked the man immediately.

Weber nodded to Royce. "Mayor."

After exchanging perfunctory handshakes, Royce

pulled out a chair for Heather, then took a seat on the other side of Mason.

"Let's get on with this, shall we?" Weber tapped a finger against his designer watch. "I have another appointment in an hour."

Heather bit the inside of her cheek to keep from telling the jerk what he could do with his other appointment. Mason didn't act intimidated by Mr. Attitude. Royce, on the other hand, looked as though he'd swallowed a handful of screws.

"This is a codicil to Mr. Henderson's will. Dated February tenth of this year." Weber slid the paper across the table.

Codicil? She and Royce exchanged glances. She waited for Mason's response, but he remained quiet, his face composed as he stared at Weber. Was he going to just sit there and let Mrs. Crawford's henchman run the show?

Royce cleared his throat. The barely discernible shake of his head warned her not to panic. Easier said than done.

Weber continued, his voice calm and assured. "In summary, the codicil states that in the event Mr. Henderson or his daughter are unable to maintain the property's upkeep, the building will be turned over to the Payton County Preservation Society."

Heather's mind reeled. What could have possessed her father to do such a thing?

Gambling. Mrs. Crawford had probably sponsored one of her father's monthly gambling trips to Louisiana in exchange for his cooperation in signing the codicil. Her father's sudden death was no doubt an unexpected but welcome surprise for the old biddy.

Mason removed his glasses and carefully set them on the table. He tented his fingers, then perched his chin on them. "I'm aware of the codicil. I discovered the document while researching the case."

"Good. After thorough investigation, Mrs. Crawford and the society feel there is enough evidence to proceed with acquiring the property." He pushed a stack of papers toward Mason. "Inspection reports clearly indicate neglect."

"Mmm-hmm." Royce's lawyer showed little interest in the reports.

Weber's brow furrowed. Obviously, he thought Mason was a real ditz. Heather wondered herself if the small-town attorney was in over his head.

"I have copies of the bank loan taken against the property earlier this week and of course the failed inspection reports."

Mason nodded. "Yes, I see."

Oh good grief! Was the man going to just sit there like a toad on a rock? She opened her mouth to speak, but swallowed the words when Royce coughed loudly and shot her a second stern warning glare. Fine. But three strikes and Mason was out.

"The codicil is signed by Robert H. Delman." Mason pointed his glasses to the signature at the bottom of the paper.

"Delman oversaw the writing of Mr. Henderson's will." Weber cleared his throat. "Moving forward. The documentation showing the store's failed inspections and inability to turn a profit—"

"Not so fast."

Heather blinked, surprised by the cold, flat tone in Mason's voice. He slipped his glasses back on his nose, then leveled a meaningful stare at Mrs. Crawford.

Heather swallowed her laughter. At least Mason was entertaining.

"In researching the case, I discovered that Mr. Delman had indeed been a practicing lawyer at the time—"

"Counsel, I don't have the faintest idea where you're going with this, but—"

"I do have a destination in mind. If you'll allow me to finish?" Mason added. "Delman was not a certified notary public as of the date on the codicil. Therefore, the codicil is invalid."

So this was it? The lawsuit against her would be dropped on a technicality?

Mrs. Crawford gasped. "That can't be." She rammed her elbow in Weber's side. "Tell them it isn't so."

"Hold on, Mason. Are you sure you want to risk a chance in court on such a small technicality?"

Heather's poor tummy couldn't handle much more of this seesawing.

"Oh, for heaven's sake. Arguing over two dead men." Mrs. Crawford stood. "I want that store, young lady."

Reining in her anger, Heather said, "Mrs. Crawford, I believe I have a right to understand why the building is so important to you."

The hot air fizzled out of the older woman and she plopped down with a *thump* in the chair. "The Payton County Preservation Society has maintained a sterling reputation over the years. We've been nominated several times for National Preservation Society of the Year. But we've yet to win." Her gaze narrowed. "Are you aware the winner of this award goes to Washington D.C. and has tea with the First Lady?"

"Tea with the First Lady sounds very exciting, but why are you targeting *my* store?"

"There has never been a registered preservation program

to turn a feed store into a museum. Private mansions, estates, schoolhouses, banks and gristmills are abundant. But to date, there is no feed store on record in this area." Her eyes narrowed. "Your building will win that award for our organization."

"But I don't want the feed store turned into a museum." How the woman thought she could bully her way to victory was beyond Heather.

"Don't be selfish, dear. You have the opportunity to make a wonderful contribution to preserve part of the history of this area and—" she cast a dark glance at Royce "—Nowhere could use the grant money to put in a much-needed sewer system."

The muscle along Royce's jaw jumped. "Nowhere's sewer problems have nothing to do with Henderson Feed Store."

"I wonder what your citizens would say, Mr. Mayor, if they had a choice in how to pay for a new sewer. Would they vote for grant money, or taxing their hard-earned dollars?"

Heather bit her tongue to keep from calling the woman a nasty name.

Royce stood. "Mrs. Crawford, you ought to know by now that I let no one and nothing threaten me into doing something I don't want to do or I don't believe is right or fair."

Sensing the growing hostility in the room, Weber stood. "This meeting is over for now." He turned to Heather with cool, assessing eyes. "Mrs. Crawford and the society have offered a very generous price for the building—considering its current financial situation and the amount of work required to salvage the structure."

Heather gave Weber her best you-can't-intimidate-me glare. "I'm not selling."

The schmuck chuckled. "We'll see about that." Weber exited the room, with Mrs. Crawford clipping his heels all the way to the door, where she stopped and faced Royce.

"I'd be careful whose side you choose, Mr. McKinnon…if you're still considering my husband's soon-to-be empty seat on the cattlemen's board." She walked out, her threat and the scent of her cloying perfume hanging heavy in the air.

Mason gathered his briefcase and stood. "Business as usual, Ms. Henderson. I'll contact you directly if there are any further developments."

She held out her hand. "Thank you very much, Mr. Mason."

"My pleasure. Royce, always good to see you."

"Thanks, Mason. Keep me up to date."

Left alone in the room, Heather flashed a victory grin. "You were right. Mason's one sharp attorney."

"Don't count on Mrs. Crawford giving up. She reminds me of a military general—retreat, regroup, attack again."

"Royce, why didn't you tell me that Mrs. Crawford's husband is the man whose seat you're thinking of running for on the cattlemen's board?"

"Because it's not important." He pushed his chair under the table. "Ready?"

"In a minute. First, I want some answers. Truthfully, how bad is the sewer?"

Folding his arms over his chest, he leaned his hips against the table edge. "Bad. The whole system needs a major overhaul. The past couple of years we've had several backups, burst pipes. As a result, a few of the stores on Main Street have suffered some damage, but nothing major. Yet."

"If the preservation society wins that national award because of my store, will Nowhere receive a grant to repair the sewer?"

He rubbed his brow. "Mrs. Crawford didn't paint you the whole picture."

"What is the whole picture?"

"The Crawford family is a big supporter of Senator Rinewall. Because of the hefty campaign donations they've handed him in the past, he's agreed to *find* funds to pay for a new sewer for the town as long as the feed store is turned over to the preservation society."

"Is that legal?"

He shrugged. "Politics."

"How long have you been aware of this?"

"The senator's aide called yesterday."

"So Mrs. Crawford made up the whole thing about a national contest?"

"The contest is real. The grant isn't."

"The witch." Heather fingered the edge of the table's smooth surface and stared at the beige carpet. Most of the people in Nowhere were hardworking citizens. No one was wealthy. Families lived in modest homes or trailers. None of them could afford higher taxes.

He tilted her chin upward. "I know what you're thinking."

"No, you don't."

In his Royce-like way, he leaned in, intending to intimidate her. "Yes, I do."

The scent of his aftershave surrounded her and she inhaled deeply, enjoying the clean, earthy smell. "Okay, then what am I thinking?"

The golden flecks in his brown eyes darkened. "You're thinking of playing superwoman and coming to the rescue of Nowhere by selling the store." He brushed an imaginary speck from her cheek, his fingers lingering to caress the sensitive skin on her neck.

"But..." She swayed forward until they bumped chests.

"I'm going to kiss you."

Surprised that he'd made the first move, Heather licked her lips in anticipation. His eyes followed the movement of her tongue as his mouth descended on hers.

His lips touched hers in the faintest caress. Clutching his suit lapels, she begged him to really kiss her—all out. Like the world was ending. Like there was no tomorrow. Only today. Only this moment. Here. Now.

A groan vibrated in his throat as he opened his mouth wider and set her soul on fire. She slid her hands up his chest and around his neck, and gave in to the urge to finger the silky hair brushing the collar of his shirt.

They shouldn't be doing this. Not here, where someone might walk in and catch her and Royce crawling all over each other. His hand clutched her hip, bringing her against his arousal. *One more kiss.*

She concentrated on the physical pleasure, the tingling sensations consuming her body, but sentiment intervened, sweetening the kiss. His embrace felt so right, so natural. So meant to be.

He was part of her past, very much a part of her present, and she yearned to make him *all* of her future. Heads tilted, noses bumped, moans and sighs mingled. His hands were everywhere at once. Her face, neck, back, waist and, finally, her bottom, where they held her firmly against him...making her very aware of how much he wanted her.

If they didn't stop, she'd pull away and start shedding her clothes. A giggle broke loose as she pictured Mrs.

Crawford stepping through the doorway and discovering her and Royce naked, squirming on top of the conference table.

Abruptly, Royce broke off the kiss, then tucked her head beneath his chin.

At least one of them was still sane.

"Heather." His throat moved against her cheek when he swallowed. "I shouldn't want you."

"Yes, you should."

He buried his face against her neck, kissing and suckling the tender skin beneath her ear.

Not wanting the pleasure to end, greedy for more, she held his head. "Follow me back to the store."

He rubbed his cheek against her hair. "I've tried to be noble, but you make it damn near impossible. I couldn't live with myself if you regretted this."

After planting one more lingering kiss on his mouth, she stepped out of his arms and led him by the hand from the room. Before they exited the building, she squeezed his fingers and whispered, "The only thing I'll regret is if you stand me up, cowboy."

Chapter Twelve

Where *was* he?

Having arrived back in Nowhere almost an hour ago, Heather waited in the lot behind the store for Royce. He'd followed her home until she'd taken the first exit to town. She'd almost run the Ford up an embankment when he continued down the highway.

Her heart had frozen for all of ten seconds, then common sense had kicked in and she'd decided he'd stopped for gas. Or maybe he'd been hungry and wanted to grab a burger at the drive-in on the highway. *Yeah, right. He chickened out.*

As the sun sank lower in the sky, she battled tears. She could make all the excuses in the world for him, but nothing would ease the sting of his rejection.

"What are you doing standing out here in the shadows?"

Gasping, she swung around. Lost in her misery, she hadn't heard Royce approach.

"Lose your key?" he asked.

He'd come. Tears dribbled from the corners of her eyes and rolled down her cheek.

He wiped the wetness away. "Tears?"

"I thought you'd changed your mind."

"Honey, I could no more leave you tonight than sell the ranch." He cupped her face. "I parked on the other side of town. It's nobody's business but ours what I'm doing here tonight."

With a hand against her back, he opened the door, then ushered her inside. When she reached for the light switch, he snagged her arm away and brought her body up against his. The storeroom was dark, casting shadows over his features. His mouth moved toward hers. Hot. Hungry. Urgent and demanding.

She'd wait an eternity if his kisses were her reward.

Shifting, he crowded her against the closed door. His hands molded her breasts and his hips thrust against her, sending sweet, aching heat surging through her body.

He broke the kiss. "I want you, Heather. I've wanted you for three long years."

She clasped his hand in hers and led him to the small room she used as her living quarters. Leaving him standing in the doorway, she switched on the reading lamp by the bed. The dim light created a romantic atmosphere. She waited by the bed, the tension in the air taut with yearning.

When he hesitated, she felt a flutter of panic. Fearing he might change his mind, she grabbed the ends of her sweater and tugged the cotton fabric over her head. His appreciative stare warmed her skin. She unfastened the buttons on her skirt, then let the material slide down her legs and pool around her feet.

Clad in a matching black-lace bra-and-panty set, she stood before him, vulnerable and needy. Eyes smoldering, he raked his gaze over her, starting at her head, slowly moving past her shoulders, stalling for a moment on her breasts, then again at her hips, before continuing down the length of her bare legs.

Daringly, she moved across the room and stopped when the tips of her satin-covered breasts rubbed against his dress shirt. Never breaking eye contact, she set his hand on the lace waistband of her panties.

One masculine finger toyed with her belly ring a moment before dipping lower and caressing her. Gasping, she thrust her hips forward, seeking that something she knew only Royce could give her. He lifted her up into his arms and deposited her on the bed.

He shed his clothes with an eagerness that brought a smile to her face. Naked, he stood before her—all muscle and masculine power. Royce was better…much better than her dreams.

"You can change your mind." His voice jolted her. "I'll leave, no questions asked."

"Never." She sat up and wrapped her arms around his waist, then rubbed her face against his stomach. With gentle hands she cupped him, stroking and caressing, wanting her touch to replace bad memories with newer, better ones. She yearned to tell him how much it hurt her to think of the pain he'd gone through. But her throat swelled shut and only a tiny sniffle escaped.

"Heather, no." He shuddered against her. "Don't cry for me." His fingers threaded through her hair, pressing her face closer.

"You should have called me. I would have come home."

"I know, honey. That's why I didn't—too much pride."

After one more lingering caress, she leaned back on the bed and held her hand out to him in invitation. He settled over her body, rubbing his muscled chest against her breasts, making her nipples tingle and harden. His mouth made love to her neck, her face and finally…*ah,* finally her breasts. After sucking her through the lace, he released the front catch on the bra, then flung the scrap across the room. "You're so beautiful, Heather." He teased her flesh, rolling the pebbled nub across his tongue, then nibbled it with his teeth.

While his lips and mouth pleasured her, his hands traveled lower. Her breath came in gasps as he edged aside the lace and caressed her intimately.

Before long, her panties were gone, too, and his mouth found her belly. When his tongue teased the butterfly ring her hips came off the bed and gyrated wildly, until his mouth moved on. He skimmed her thighs, her knees, her ankles and…oh my…he suckled her toes!

Easing himself away, he snatched his pants from the floor and rummaged through the pockets.

Oh. He was looking for a condom. How like the Royce she loved. He might be sterile, but he wanted to protect her from other concerns, as well.

She slid around in front of him and helped with the condom, then went up on tiptoes and kissed him, while her hand traveled south. Taking her time, she made him forget everything but the feel of her touch.

Soon, touching and kissing weren't enough. He tumbled her to the bed pressing her to the mattress, and murmured what he planned to do to her soon.

Eagerly, she opened her legs in invitation.

"Not yet," he whispered in her ear.

His mouth left a glistening trail of moisture as he worked his way down her body once again. He kissed the inside of each thigh until she whimpered and begged.

"Please, Royce. Please."

"Please what, honey?" He nuzzled the little butterfly.

"Kiss me," she panted.

His hands curled around her bottom and lifted her hips off the bed.

Heather trembled, surrendering to his hot, searching mouth. She begged. She whimpered. She cried out as a powerful force sent her off into her own private world of bliss.

Before she'd even caught her breath, he moved over her, fitting his hips snugly in the cradle of her thighs. "One more time, babe."

Barely able to move a muscle, she moaned, "I can't."

"I like challenges." He entered her slow and easy, his eyes searching her face. "Okay?"

"Mmm. More than okay." She dug her nails into his shoulders and held him prisoner with her legs. Her heart swelled with love and awe at her being one with Royce.

Tears burned the backs of her eyes, and he kissed her dewy lashes. "You're so damn incredible, Heather. I never thought it would feel this perfect." He rested his forehead against hers, holding himself still.

His confession gladdened her heart. Made her yearn to admit her love for him, even though she sensed he didn't want to hear the words.

After a moment, he moved gently. Sparks flickered to life in her belly. She shifted, meeting him thrust for thrust. In a matter of seconds, they set a wild rhythm neither could control.

When she felt the touch of his hand between her thighs, she strained for the heavens once again. The first wave of her second climax stunned her. She cried out against the intense pain-pleasure, barely aware of Royce's shout as he stiffened and buried his face between her breasts.

ROYCE PULLED HEATHER CLOSE to his side and burrowed his nose in her sweet-scented hair. Her foot inched across his hairy calf, then she nestled her leg intimately between his thighs.

They'd been resting only a few minutes, but already he wanted her again. He doubted he'd ever stop needing Heather. "Are you all right?"

"Mmm. Very all right."

Relief eased the knots in his muscles. He'd been afraid that the knowledge of his sterility might somehow lessen her pleasure. Like a romantic fool, he wished time could stand still. For a little while, anyway. Long enough to convince Heather that he could make her happy…despite not being able to give her babies.

He thought about the future. What would happen after Heather earned her degree? Where would her first job be—nearby or far away? Would working with disadvantaged children be enough to fill the void in a childless marriage? After a few years, would her biological clock chime? What then? Would she end up leaving him to fulfill the one dream he couldn't make happen for her?

Ask her to stay. Ask her to give you a chance to make her happy.

Needing to catch his breath, he swung his legs over the side of the bed, then stood and moved across the room. Keeping his back to her, he braced his hands against the door frame and bowed his head. *Damn it.* Where was that confident, take-charge guy Heather always complained about?

Emotions he wasn't comfortable with warred inside him, seizing his heart. Anger at the unfairness of life. Sorrow for the lost children he'd never father. Doubt that he could hold on to the woman he'd given his heart to.

HEATHER TUGGED the end of the bedsheet until the fabric came loose, then wrapped herself in the soft cotton—the flimsy barrier hardly a shield against the dark thoughts she sensed in her lover's mind. "Royce?"

He glanced over his shoulder, his eyes turbulent.

She stepped closer, but froze when he winced. They'd just shared the most incredible experience—and he regretted it?

He faced her. "This isn't going to last."

"And you believe that because…?"

"Once you get your degree you'll spread your wings and fly off. Get that dream job counseling kids."

Ah, now I understand. "My working with kids would be a problem for you?" She hoped he could see that her love for him was strong enough to carry them through the rough patches.

"In time you might need more out of life than a career and…me."

His stoic posture unnerved her, tumbled her off balance. Then his shoulders sagged as if he couldn't carry the weight of his feelings any longer. "You deserve only the best."

A lump rose in her throat, but she swallowed it down. "Would you believe me if I said *you* are best for me?"

His yearning expression convinced her that he wanted to believe her but lacked the guts. She was both hurt and angry. Only a few feet separated them, but the emotional distance might as well have been miles.

Well, she could be just as stubborn as him. She'd stick around Nowhere until he found the courage to accept her love.

"In the long run it wouldn't work between us, Heather."

"Why?"

"We're not compatible."

Of all the silly... "How are we not compatible? Just a few minutes ago we got along quite well."

He lifted his pants from the floor and pulled them on. "For one—" he gestured at the small room "—you're messy."

Not much to deny there. She had a week's worth of dirty laundry strewn about the floor, an open bag of pretzels on the nightstand and a leaning tower of books and papers behind the door. "True." She edged closer. "How else?"

He pulled the pant zipper up and glared at her. "I'm conservative."

"I'm liberal."

He grunted. "I'm old-fashioned."

"I'm modern."

"I'm set in my ways."

"I'm adaptable." She slid a finger inside the waistband of his slacks. "You forgot your underwear."

He glanced at his briefs, which were lying under the bedside table. "Why are you making this so hard?"

Running the palm of her hand up his chest, she whispered, "I won't let you believe something so right and beautiful can't last."

He grabbed her by the shoulders and gave her a shake. "Don't you understand? I couldn't live with you waking up one morning admitting that you were wrong. That you *do* want a baby."

The anguish in his eyes jolted her. It had cost him a lot to admit his fear.

"If the time comes when I feel I want a baby of my own

to raise, then we can discuss adoption." Tired of talking, she let go of the sheet, then tugged at his zipper. His gaze followed the path of her finger and he sucked in his stomach when her knuckles grazed his aroused flesh.

Wrapping a hand around her neck, he pulled her near. His kiss led them right back to bed, which was where Heather had intended they go all along.

This time, an edge of desperation spurred their lovemaking. She attempted to evade his kisses in the hope of drawing out the experience, but he refused to cooperate. He devoured her mouth and flesh, scorching her skin, teasing her senses.

Only when she begged him to end her torture did he finally relent and give them both what they craved.

TICK, TOCK.

Tick, tock.

With each passing second, the ticking clock and the beating of his heart melded, becoming louder, more frightening, until his chest threatened to explode.

Concentrating on the shadows in the room, he fought to ignore the panic squeezing his ribs. Heather snuggled against his side, her warm, bewitching scent filling his nostrils, making him hope for things that could never be.

She scared the hell out of him—because he couldn't stop himself from taking what she offered.

He rose up on one elbow and studied her. A mass of tangled blond hair spread across the pillow. With trembling fingers, he picked up a thick lock and pressed it to his mouth.

Her passionate enthusiasm for his lovemaking had amazed him. Never had a woman seemed to crave his touch the way Heather had. And the feeling hadn't been one-sided. Her mouth and hands had teased and taunted until he'd lost himself in her over and over through the night.

Man, how he wished he could wake up in her arms each morning for the rest of his life…to hear her sleepy voice in his ear, to see the tender smile that could bring him to his knees.

Who was he kidding? A relationship with Heather was doomed from the beginning. Tenderness swept through him as he remembered the sight of her on the day-care floor, buried beneath a pile of laughing preschoolers. Although she'd had a rough childhood, he believed without a doubt that she would make a fantastic mother. And she deserved every bit of love a child would give in return.

He should have resisted her. Fought harder against his physical desire. But his attraction to her had to do with her personality, not just her body. Her zest for life was contagious. He envied her the ability to find joy in mundane tasks like sweeping the floor or delivering orders to customers. She humbled him with her genuine concern for people and unfailing determination to persevere when others would have quit. Her blue eyes sparkled with a healthy inner spirit, reeling him in with their warm and welcoming glow.

College had offered Heather the opportunity to find herself and discover who she really was—a bright, intelligent, beautiful woman. Would she stay that way if she lived with him in Nowhere forever?

He must have dozed off, because the next time he glanced at the bedside clock it was seven a.m. After a night of strenuous lovemaking he felt foggy headed. He wasn't positive, but he thought he had a meeting with someone at nine. He'd better haul his butt out of bed before that someone came looking for him and found him in Heather's arms.

Careful not to disturb her, he left the bed, gathered up his clothes and his shoes, then slipped from the room. After dressing by the back door, he shoved his hands through his hair, trying to make order of the damage Heather's fingers had done during the night. He slid the bolt free, stepped into the early-morning light and—

As if someone had landed a punch to his midsection, his breath froze in his lungs. Ten feet away, Nowhere's three town-council members were gathered with none other than Mrs. Crawford, her pinched face at the front of the pack.

So much for sneaking out.

"Is it true, Royce? If Heather sells Henderson Feed Store to the preservation society, Nowhere will get a new sewer system?" Ellen Simms, the owner of the Five and Dime Discount at the edge of town, moved forward.

How the hell did everyone know he was at the feed store, when his truck was parked across town?

Fred wiped his hand on the white barber towel slung over his shoulder. "We saw your truck down by the stationery store and figured you were over here."

Well, that answered his question. "I see you've been busy since last night's meeting, Mrs. Crawford." Obviously, she'd made a few calls and stirred up an ant's hill of trouble.

She arched a perfectly painted-on charcoal eyebrow. "Not as busy as you…apparently."

Ignoring the heat rushing up his neck, he stared down the pack of hungry wolves. "I don't know what Mrs. Crawford told you—"

"Royce." Barbershop Fred cleared his throat. "If there's a way to pay for the sewer system without raising taxes, I think we ought to consider the opportunity."

"I agree." Harold Pulaski, the bank president, tugged at his necktie. "The bank went out on a limb extending the deadline for loans after that blister beetle infestation a while back. If you tax these folks, they'll default on their payments, and the bank will have no choice but to foreclose on properties."

Royce leaned back, bumping into the half-open door. For an instant, he experienced the same panic the victim of a mob attack must feel. "Before any rumors start, I'll schedule a meeting for Monday afternoon and we'll discuss the sewer situation."

Mrs. Crawford dug through her purse and removed a planner and pen. "I'm available anytime after two."

Pinning her with a cold stare, Royce added, "The meeting's closed to the public."

Ellen worried her lower lip. "If Mrs. Crawford is part of the solution to the sewer problem, she should be present."

The whole world was spinning out of control, and Royce couldn't do a blasted thing but stand back and watch all hell break loose. "If there is anything Mrs. Crawford needs to know after the meeting, I'll contact her. See you at the bank Monday."

Fred waved his towel. "Hold up. Shouldn't Heather be there?"

"Shouldn't Heather be where?" Heather stepped through the back door wrapped in the bedsheet, hair tousled, lips swollen. She looked like a sexy, well-ravished harlot.

Mrs. Crawford gaped. Ellen giggled. And Pulaski coughed. Sliding sideways, Royce blocked Heather from view. "Get back inside," he growled over his shoulder.

"Why?" Heather murmured behind his back.

Was she nuts or just plain bullheaded? The beginning of a pounding migraine sprang behind his eyes. "You're not wearing any clothes."

She glanced down. "I'm wearing a sheet."

Eyes gleaming with victory, Mrs. Crawford taunted, "I'm sure those with influence over the cattlemen's board would be interested in hearing about your relationship with Ms. Henderson."

Royce gave Heather his full attention. "For God's sake, get back inside."

She wrinkled her nose, then retreated into the store. To be safe, he leaned against the door, making sure she couldn't poke her head out again. He glowered at each member of the council. "My relationship with Heather is private. I expect it to stay private. Understood?"

Three heads bobbed. He bit his tongue to keep from calling all three good citizens liars. By the end of the day the whole town would hear he'd slept with Heather.

Fred grumbled something as he walked away.

Ellen grinned, and Royce swore he saw the ghostly outline of wedding bells over her head.

Harold approached and mumbled, "I've been in your shoes before, Royce. Not a place a man wants to be caught twice."

A moment later, only Mrs. Crawford remained. "Mr. McKinnon, you have to agree this is a win-win situation for all involved."

"How so, ma'am?"

"First of all, I'll win the national award and the trip to Washington. Your town will receive a new sewer and you'll win my husband's vacant seat on the cattlemen's board."

"Tell me, Mrs. Crawford, if Heather sells the store, what does she win?"

"Enough money to travel far away from here. To places a country girl can only dream of."

Exactly what Royce feared.

Chapter Thirteen

"Mind telling me what that was all about out there?"

Heather wasn't fooled by the deceptively calm tone in Royce's voice. The rigid line of his jaw, his stiff shoulders and his fists all worked together to create a picture of one hundred-percent pure hostile male.

While he'd fended off the gossipmongers out back, she'd washed up, slipped on a sundress and a pair of sandals, then flipped the window sign at the front of the store to Open. She'd just returned to the back counter, when Royce came inside. A little voice in her head warned her to tread lightly.

"I'm not sure what you mean."

He moved closer, backing her up until her hips bumped the counter. Desire rushed through her blood as his scent—faded aftershave and earthy male—threatened to scramble her thoughts. She studied his unshaven face, her breasts tingling at the memory of those abrasive whiskers rubbing her sensitive skin.

"You flaunted yourself like a damn Jezebel out there."

Heather battled a smile when she spotted the stubborn lock of hair that stood up on the back of his head. "The whole town will know by supper that we've slept together."

She felt a pang of regret. Royce was a private man and her going outside in nothing but a bedsheet had been a heck of a shock to his system. She should have contented herself with hiding behind the door and eavesdropping. But presenting herself had been a knee-jerk reaction. She'd been talked about behind her back most of her life. When she heard her name, she acted without thinking.

Aside from a healthy dose of guilt, an equal amount of hurt filled her. Royce's angry reaction had her assuming he regretted that their relationship would soon be public knowledge. "Are you embarrassed they found out we made love last night?"

His mouth thinned. "What we do behind closed doors is nobody's business but ours."

That he'd neatly sidestepped the question hadn't escaped her. The tension between them grew tauter by the second. "Do you?"

His gaze narrowed. "Do I what?"

"Regret sleeping with me." She thrust her chin in the air, hoping to hide the aching need for him that she feared showed in her eyes. Making love with him had been the most wonderful thing she'd ever experienced. In her heart and mind she believed last night was the beginning of a serious, hopefully lifelong relationship with Royce.

His dark eyes unnerved her and she wondered if he was trying to see into her soul. "Right now, I think we could both use a little breathing room."

Speak for yourself.

Neither stirred—as if one false move might trigger an emotional eruption that would engulf them both.

She hesitated only a second before throwing a lit match on the already smoldering fire between them. "Ignoring me won't keep you from wanting me again, Royce."

Reacting out of fear and a sense of time running out, she closed the gap between them. She pressed her breasts to his chest, determined to convince him that he needed her. Shameless or not, she'd use her body to buy more time, until he admitted that what he felt for her had a whole lot more to do with love than lust.

She raised her mouth to his, and their breaths mingled for less than a second before his mouth crushed hers, forcing her lips apart, searching with his tongue. His hands held her head immobile and she could do little else but stand before him, absorbing the sheer force of his kiss.

When he came up for air, she counterattacked and followed his mouth with her own, thrusting her tongue inside with daring accuracy. The tremor that shook his body spurred her on, and she boldly ran her hands down his chest, buttons popping in their wake.

When her fingers reached his belt buckle he clasped them in an iron grip. "Stop." His heavy breathing pulsed against her neck. "Time, Heather. Give me time to think about this."

If she gave him time, he'd run and she'd never catch him. "I love you, Royce."

His body jerked before he dropped her hands and moved away. Not the reaction she'd hoped for. Fighting tears, she waited for a word, a gesture, anything that would prove her heartfelt declaration meant *something* to him. After an eternity, he gathered her back into the shelter of his body.

Sniffing, she hugged him. He had no idea of the havoc he caused in her heart. She'd taken a gamble in confessing her love for him. Her admission might backfire and drive him away for good. But it was sweet relief to declare what her heart had realized for weeks.

And she wasn't so naive as to believe that simply loving him would fix their relationship. If only she knew how to convince him she wanted him for the long haul.

"You're making this so damn hard, honey," he muttered against her neck.

Not the profession of undying love she'd hoped for. Clutching his shirtsleeve, she led the way back to the storeroom…into a dark corner. There, fueled by equal parts anger at his stubbornness and desperation, she backed him up against the brick wall and made quick work of unzipping his pants. She reached inside and released him, then went down on her knees. His fingers bit into her shoulders and she heard the quiet *thunk* of his head hitting the wall. Feeling empowered, she lavished her attention on him. But her own pleasure in pleasing him was short-lived.

He yanked her up and reversed their positions. Now *her* back was to the wall.

The bell above the front door jingled, and they both froze.

He watched her, waiting for her to decide. In answer to his unspoken question, she ran her tongue across his lips.

Shoving her dress up her thighs, he moved her panties to one side and drove inside her. He pressed his open mouth to her neck and moaned.

She clutched his shoulders, then clamped her legs around his waist. He slid deeper and she closed her eyes, allowing the tension building between them to sweep her away.

Their road to fulfillment wasn't pretty, wasn't filled with soft loving touches or quiet kisses. It was hard, hot and so intense she bit his shoulder to keep from screaming her release out loud.

The customer service bell on the counter clanged twice.

With shaking hands he set her from him and straightened her dress, then rubbed his thumb across her swollen lips. Without meeting her eyes, he motioned toward the door and whispered, "Go."

She slid around him, but paused at the doorway and glanced over her shoulder. She wished she hadn't.

Head bowed in defeat, Royce pounded his fist against the wall.

A BLAST OF REFRIGERATED AIR stole her breath when Heather entered Loyalty Savings and Loan on Monday afternoon. The fact that Royce hadn't extended an invitation to the impromptu council meeting hadn't deterred her from attending.

Hesitating a moment, she allowed her eyes to adjust to the interior lighting, then she headed for the manager's office, located in the back of the bank. Halfway across the foyer, she noticed the teller's eyes on her. She imagined the grapevine was humming with juicy gossip about her and Royce. Good grief, didn't these people have better things to do than talk about her and Royce's sex life?

Squaring her shoulders, she continued through the lobby toward Harold Pulaski's office. She rapped twice on the closed door before walking in unannounced.

Four sets of startled eyes greeted her. "Excuse me." She avoided Royce's gaze, instead seeking out Ellen, whose gentle expression seemed more welcoming at the moment. "I believe I have a right to be here, since my store is smack-dab in the middle of this controversy."

Royce stood by a window, while Fred and Ellen sat in front of Harold's desk. Except for the blush on his poker-straight face, Royce showed no irritation at her intrusion.

Harold scooted his black leather chair back and stood. "Ms. Henderson—"

"This meeting is for town-council members only." Royce shifted away from his post by the window.

Heather jumped at the sharp note in Royce's voice. She wasn't the only one affected by his outburst. Perhaps suspecting he was about to witness a lovers' quarrel, Harold suddenly took interest in reading a file from his In basket, Fred grabbed a fishing magazine from the table next to him and Ellen rummaged through her purse.

"I'm staying."

She swallowed hard at the "we'll talk about this later" expression on his face. No doubt he'd find a way to exact revenge for her butting in where she wasn't welcome.

Ellen motioned to the empty chair nearby. Heather slid onto the seat cushion, ignoring the trio of loud exhales that reverberated through the room.

Giving Ellen his attention, Royce asked, "Did you bring the latest inspection reports on the sewer?"

The older woman nodded, her salt-and-pepper hair swinging across her face. She handed out copies of the report and the room quieted as each person scanned them.

The information shocked Heather. That every toilet in Nowhere hadn't backed up, flooding the sidewalks and streets, was a miracle. "How did the sewer deteriorate to this level without anybody being aware?" Immediately, she regretted the hasty question. She hadn't meant to criticize Royce's mayoral performance, but the wounded look in his eyes told her he'd taken offense at her remark.

Royce cleared his throat. "We've been aware for over four years now that the whole system is in need of a major overhaul."

"Then—"

"Money, Ms. Henderson." Harold tapped the eraser end of a pencil against his desk blotter. "Money. Money. Money."

"We pay too many taxes as it is," Fred grumbled.

Harold glanced at Royce, then shook his head. "We don't have a big enough tax base to support something of this magnitude." He directed his next words to Heather. "We can't raise taxes. The community is made up largely of ranchers, who are still recouping their losses from insect disease, floods and droughts over the past eight years."

"What about federal loans or grant monies?" Heather tossed the question out to no one in particular. There had to be a way the town could acquire financing for something as necessary as a sewage system.

Ellen shifted in her chair. "We applied two years ago for a government grant and received a letter back saying we qualified."

For the first time since the discussion began, Heather felt a flicker of hope.

"But—" Ellen smiled sadly "—we're far down on the list."

"How far down?"

"There are seventeen towns ahead of us in the state of Texas. I'm not sure where we rank nationally."

Heather rubbed her forehead. The situation was growing worse by the second.

As if sensing her anxiety, the storekeeper patted her hand. "We've tried everything we can think of. Royce has written several letters to our congressman. He's even taken a trip to Austin to speak to the governor."

Turning her attention to Royce, she held his gaze, not caring if the others saw the love she felt for him shining in her eyes. His relentless determination to fight for his people filled her with pride. Understanding the type of man he was, she sensed he saw his inability to solve the sewer dilemma as a personal failure.

"What about that private funding you said you were gonna check into?" Fred asked.

Royce's mouth turned down. "Dalton Industries declined the invitation to open a plant outside of Nowhere. I haven't heard back from Kempler Transit yet."

The silence in the room stretched, and Heather assumed all of them were busy racking their brains for a solution. The situation appeared bleak. Worse than bleak: impossible. The council needed a knight in shining armor to rescue their fair town.

A picture of Mrs. Crawford's face flashed before Heather's eyes. Now she understood why the woman's proposal to buy her store sounded like a dream come true to the members of the council.

"All right. The next step is to attack repairing the sewer one section at a time." Royce motioned to the report. "The section labeled 3C, located right under Main Street, is the worst. Ellen, compile three estimates and get them to me by this Thursday if not sooner."

"But there're more bad spots." Fred waved the report in the air.

"The rest of the sewer should hold up through the winter. Next spring we'll tackle another section and maybe by summer we'll have moved to the top of the list for government funding."

Harold shook his head. "That's quite a gamble."

"True. But it proves to the citizens we're *trying* to do something without raising their taxes. In the meantime, we'll keep up the advertising campaign to attract industry to the area." Royce moved toward the door, his final comments ending the meeting.

Fred bolted from his seat. "But we haven't discussed the other option."

All eyes turned to Heather. Suddenly, it became clear why she hadn't been invited to the meeting.

"There is no other option, Fred," Royce insisted.

Ignoring Royce's warning glare, the barber blurted, "What about Mrs. Crawford's proposal to buy out Ms. Henderson?"

"No one in this room is going to sit here and pressure Heather into selling. Besides, the grant is bogus. A cover-up for dirty political monies."

Fred sat down, frowning at the tips of his shoes.

"I think it should be noted that there is always a chance Ms. Henderson will default on the loan she took out with the bank in Blairdsville." Harold leaned back in his chair. "If that happens, the bank will sell to Mrs. Crawford and the preservation society and walk away with a tidy profit. Heather still loses the store, but Nowhere gains nothing."

The banker's statement was edged with hostility, and Heather's ire rose. "I won't be defaulting on the loan, Mr. Pulaski."

"Can we be honest here, Ms. Henderson?" Harold's expression grew stormy.

"By all means. Let's be honest." *Jerk.*

He stretched his arms across the desk blotter. "With you at the helm of Henderson Feed, the odds of making a success of the business are slim. Next to nil."

Royce moved behind Heather's chair. "That's enough, Harold."

"Let him speak his mind," Heather insisted, grateful for Royce's support.

"You don't exactly have a stellar past in this town, Ms. Henderson. How do we know this urge to run the feed store isn't just a temporary amusement until something more interesting comes along?"

"Heather's done nothing to deserve that kind of disrespect from you, Harold. She's worked her tail off, and the feed-store improvements have reflected positively on the town."

The banker's cheeks puffed up like a bullfrog's. "Aren't we being a little biased? Wasn't that you sneaking out her back door three mornings ago?"

Fury flashed in Royce's eyes. "My relationship with Heather is none of your business." He glanced around the group. "Have I ever allowed anything or anyone to interfere with my duties as mayor of Nowhere?" Ellen and Fred shook their heads. "The day I don't have the well-being of the town's citizens in mind you can toss me out of office."

Having his integrity questioned was an affront Royce rarely, if ever, experienced. Heather didn't care about the snide remarks Harold directed at her. She'd lived with talk like that all her life and had learned to let those kinds of comments roll off her back. But it angered her that Pulaski had so little respect for a man who had unselfishly served them for the past two years.

Hoping to prevent the thundercloud forming over Royce's head from bursting, she butted in. "My relationship with the mayor is private. I understand that may be worrisome, but I assure you my intentions toward him are honorable."

Four stunned faces stared at her. Then Ellen snickered. Fred chortled into his fist. And the corners of Harold's mouth twitched. Royce rolled his eyes and strode back to his post by the window.

The tension in the room dissolved, and Heather was relieved she wouldn't have to bail Royce out of jail for slugging the bank president.

Ellen sighed. "We don't mean to pry or be rude, Heather. But if there's any chance at all you won't be able to succeed with the feed store or that you'll eventually leave town...well, we believe the preservation society offer may be the best solution for everyone."

The walls closed in around Heather. Her insides twisted and churned. No one, not even Royce, believed she'd stick around Nowhere forever. Queasy, she murmured, "I guess I have some thinking to do."

Fred nodded. "Seems like a win-win situation for everyone, if you ask me. You'll get some pocket change, the society gets their feed store and Nowhere gets a new sewer."

Royce frowned. "For now, let's sit tight."

Bunching up his face like a petulant child, Fred grumbled, "Until the sewer explodes and we got poop floating down the middle of the street?"

"Shush!" Ellen smacked Fred's thigh with her purse.

"Meeting's over, folks." Royce motioned to the door. Fred, Ellen and even Harold filed out of the office.

Heather offered a tight smile. "That went real well."

"What did you expect? This is small-town America. People here see things as either right or wrong. Black or white. Hot or cold. They don't look at the whole picture, nor do they want to." He rubbed his eyes and grimaced. The past forty minutes had taken a toll on him.

She wanted to lean on him if only for a few seconds, but he already had enough responsibilities weighing him down. "I'll give some thought to selling the store to the preservation society."

"Mrs. Crawford's offer is very generous. You'd have a nest egg to fall back on after graduation."

Did he want her to stay or leave? Trying to read the truth in his carefully blank face was useless. His face remained carefully blank. "I suppose a little extra rainy-day money would come in handy."

"The cash would help you get settled in a place where you can put your degree to work."

She had planned on looking for a job nearby Nowhere in one of the neighboring towns along the interstate. "Will you be stopping by the store later tonight?"

Longing flashed through his eyes, then he turned his attention to something outside the window. "No."

Just like that. He was determined to end their relationship before it had even gotten off the ground.

Well, two could play the stubborn game.

"DONE."

Heather moved the arrow to Send and clicked. What a relief. One term paper down, one to go. At least the professor had agreed to receive the report via an e-mail attachment instead of a paper copy through the mail. The man ought to be lenient, since he'd upped the due date.

As she shut down the laptop, she hummed along to the tune of a Top 40 song blaring from the radio in her private quarters. Now that her paper was finished, thoughts of the feed store's financial situation and the meeting at the bank earlier in the day filled her mind. After grabbing a can of soda from the fridge and the stack of bills from beneath the counter, she went out the front door and sat on the steps.

The moon, high and bright in the sky, cast shadows against the buildings up and down the deserted street. Moist night air enveloped her, and the scent of the lavender in the planter at the bottom of the steps wafted under her nose.

Mentally calculating the debts, she divided the envelopes into three piles: urgent, more urgent and most urgent. No matter how she added things up, the number in the thousands column remained the same. Six thousand dollars—which didn't include back taxes or the new loan payment for the plumbing and electrical upgrades. She could no longer turn her head and hope the numbers would decrease the next time she checked.

Who was she kidding? General day-to-day business didn't bring in enough money to pay down on the debt, let alone enough to pay for the daily operating expenses. If the preservation society continued to demand upgrades and improvements to the building, she didn't have a chance in hell of staying afloat. Not one bank this side of the Mississippi would give her a second loan.

She considered the meager two hundred dollars left in her personal savings account. She'd be eating peanut-butter-and-jelly sandwiches for the next six months—if the store didn't go bankrupt first. The idea of losing the business stung her pride. The numbers on the bills blurred before her eyes and the feather-light envelopes felt like chunks of cement in her hand. Sometimes being an adult just plain sucked.

Operating the feed store in the red was not a sound business decision. The bills proved that adults needed to know when to cut their losses and walk away. She had to consider all her options. Not that she had many, except for selling the place to Mrs. Crawford and the preservation society.

The thought of that old, fire-breathing dragon getting

her hands on the store made the short hairs on the back of Heather's neck stand straight up.

She needed a miracle. And so did the town of Nowhere.

An image of Royce's face floated through her mind. He sure tested her resolve. Maybe she should sell the store and kiss the cranky cattleman's rusty spurs goodbye. After all, he wanted her to give up, didn't he?

But something inside her refused to make things that easy for him. Admitting she loved the rancher was the easy part. How to convince him her love was a mature, forever kind of love was proving more difficult.

Time was her enemy. If she didn't keep the business afloat, she'd have no reason to stay in Nowhere and continue trying to convince Royce they were meant to spend the rest of their lives together.

The sound of a diesel motor broke the night silence. She watched Royce's black Dodge swing around the corner. He slowed to a stop at the curb in front of the store, lowered the driver's window and cut the ignition.

There was just enough moonlight to see inside the cab. She smothered a smile behind a discreet cough at the sight of his rigid posture. Lord, the man was hard on himself. If only he'd admit his love for her, he could stop wearing himself out, fighting the attraction between them.

"Hello, Royce. Nice evening for a drive." The giggle crawling up her throat squeaked past her closed lips.

His eyes flashed with irritation.

Getting a rise out of him was more fun than going to a college pep rally. "There's plenty of room here on the step. Come sit a spell."

He opened the door and unfolded his tall body from the front seat. Hesitating at the curb, he rubbed his palms down the front of his jeans-clad thighs. Hatless, his burnished hair looked almost black in the moonlight.

She patted the spot next to her. "Take a load off, cowboy."

One corner of his mouth twitched as his long strides ate up the distance between them. He sat, a good two feet from her. She shifted, closing the gap considerably.

Her skin tingled when his jeans rubbed against her bare leg. The strong scent of cologne had her believing he'd splashed some on before coming to see her, and she inched even closer. As a matter of fact, the ends of his hair were damp. Closing her eyes, she envisioned his powerful body standing in the shower, his hands soaping his chest, his stomach, his—"

"I think you should sell the store."

"Huh?" She shook her head, the naked image of Royce scattering to the four corners of her mind.

"Hear me out."

"But—"

"Please, Heather. Listen first, okay?"

If he had demanded she listen, she would have stormed back inside and left him sitting by his lonesome on the stoop. But he'd asked so nicely, so sincerely, she couldn't refuse. "Okay, I'm all ears."

"Advising you to sell to the preservation society has nothing to do with getting a new sewer for the town."

The honesty in his eyes begged her to believe him. There was no question in her mind that Royce had her best interests at heart. "I believe you, Royce."

"The town council never should have pressured you."

"I'm not upset about that." She fingered his T-shirt sleeve. "I liked being a part of the community for a change." She winked. "Even if I am one of their problems."

"You're not a problem." He tucked a strand of her hair behind her ear. "I admire how hard you've worked to make a go of the business. I knew better than anyone the challenges you faced when you took over the store." A reluctant smile curved his mouth. "I admit you surprised the heck out of me when you didn't tuck tail and run after the first week."

Heather's heart ached with love for the man.

Taking her hand in his, he caressed her fingers one by one. Not the action she'd expect from a man who supposedly had ended things between them earlier in the day. "I should have told you a lot sooner. Better late than never, I guess."

"Told me what?" The way he played with her fingers short-circuited her central nervous system.

"Told you how proud I am of you."

Her throat clogged with emotion. "Thank you for telling me."

Several minutes passed before he released her hand. "I understand you need to handle things your own way, but after talking with Harold again, I don't see how you'll be able to pay on the loan and keep the store open for business much longer."

"Whether I succeed or fail is up to me. Not you."

His chuckle sounded strangled. "Letting you go out on a limb alone isn't easy, Heather. God, I wish it were. For your sake and mine."

Hope flickered in her chest. She snuck her arm around his waist and rested her head on his shoulder. "Let me worry about the store. One way or another, everything will work out." *For the store. For us. Maybe even for Nowhere.*

"Too many things are stacked against you for you to succeed."

"I've faced worse odds before."

"The preservation society's offer is more than generous."

"So you've said." She picked at an imaginary speck on his thigh. "If I lose the store…I lose the store. I won't become destitute. I'm capable of getting a job and taking care of myself."

He lifted her chin. "You don't have to convince me you're capable of taking care of yourself."

Good. Let me convince you that I'm capable of loving you.

He loved her, darn it! Why wouldn't he admit his feelings? Why wouldn't he accept her love?

"We discussed the store. Now tell me why you really came here tonight."

"I don't know what you mean."

"I never pegged you for a coward, Royce."

"You want blood, don't you."

"I want the truth. Out in the open between us."

"Damn you, Heather. You're tearing me up inside."

"You're doing a reasonable amount of damage to me, too."

He pulled her close, his mouth barely an inch from hers. "You want to know why I came tonight?" His fingers tightened in her hair. "I came because I couldn't get your scent out of my head. I can't shut my eyes without seeing your face, your sexy, naked body under mine. Nothing tastes good anymore because I can't get the flavor of you out of my mouth. Is that enough, or do you want to hear more?"

His mouth crashed down on hers, his tongue parting her lips, claiming her, ravishing her, seducing her until she had to clutch his shirtsleeves to keep from collapsing in the lavender planter.

Abruptly, his kiss changed—softening, sipping at her

lips, the corners of her mouth. His tongue stroked, his teeth nibbled, his nose nuzzled.

The tenderness brought tears to her eyes. When he pulled back, he rested his forehead against hers and slowly released his death grip on her hair. He smoothed the errant strands back in place, then set her aside and hopped down the steps toward his truck. He swung the door open but paused before getting in.

"The preservation society informed me that you have five days to accept or reject their offer before they resume legal action."

Heather *really, really* didn't like Mrs. Crawford.

"Are you going to sell out, Heather?"

Heather had a sneaking suspicion that Royce wasn't talking about the store…but about their relationship.

Chapter Fourteen

"Who was that, Heather?" Royce motioned over his shoulder at the man who'd just left the store.

"My guardian angel." She smiled, refusing to let the frown on Royce's face put a damper on her high spirits. Stepping around the counter, she met him in the fencing aisle.

"Seemed pretty citified to me."

"He ought to. He's from Austin." She was so excited she was about to bust the seams of her tight denim shorts.

"Long way to come for feed supplies."

She grinned. "If I didn't know better, I'd think you were jealous." Whirling away, she headed for the storeroom, Royce hounding her heels like a disgruntled dog.

"Actually, he's going to be buying more than feed." She flipped on the light.

Royce stopped in the doorway and leaned a shoulder against the jamb. "What's that supposed to mean?"

She wondered if his hesitancy in following her farther into the room had anything to do with memories of their sexy tryst against the back wall. "Do you have a minute?"

"All day."

Glancing at the bed in her living quarters, she contemplated enticing him inside and encouraging him to put all that pent-up frustration to good use. "The man's name is Richard Cain. His family's been in the feed-supply business in Austin for fifty years. You may have heard of Cain Livestock Supply?"

Royce nodded.

"Well. That's neither here nor there, I guess."

"Heather. Skip the details and cut to the chase."

Touchy, touchy. "After I arrived in town back in June, I sent out several letters to feed-store suppliers and businesses throughout Texas. I stated my interest in forming an alliance of—"

"You did what?" He moved a threatening step forward. "Do you have any idea how you've opened yourself up for—"

"Wait." He did, and it caught her by such surprise she almost forgot what she'd been about to say. "I received a couple letters of interest, but nothing evolved from any of them. Then last week Richard Cain phoned and asked to set up a meeting today."

"Why didn't you tell me about the meeting?"

Anger sharpened her response. "You haven't been an easy man to get a hold of." *And you never return my calls.* The miserable man had been avoiding her. The last time she'd seen Royce was over a week ago when he'd pulled up in his truck in front of the store. Since then, July had turned to August. Mrs. Crawford had notified her that she would continue to pursue legal action. Heather had defaulted on her first loan payment. And…she'd finished her final term paper. Life went on—with or without Royce.

"Just like that, you're letting this Cain guy buy into the store?"

Irritated, she snapped her fingers in the air. "Just like that."

"Have you checked their company's financial records? Hell, Heather, his business could be in worse shape than yours. He might leave you bankrupt."

"Bankrupt? I'm halfway there already."

He whipped his hat off his head. "Why didn't you discuss this with me first?" He didn't allow her to answer before he fired off another question. "How am I supposed to watch out for you if you go behind my back all the time?"

"I didn't go behind your back." She resented the insinuation that she was sneaky. "How many times do I have to repeat myself—the store isn't *your* problem." His mouth turned down into a sulk. Ignoring him, she continued. "Richard is willing to pay off the back taxes and front the money to finish the repairs the preservation society insists I have to make in order to keep the building. He's also willing to put up the money to enlarge and update my inventory."

"What percentage of the store will he own when you sign on the dotted line?"

"Sixty-five percent."

The snort out of Royce's mouth sailed through the air and smacked her sideways. "Might as well hand the whole place over to him right now."

Ignoring his nastiness—*again*—she added, "Richard's parents want to retire. Health problems, I think. They have a cabin close by on Lake Wright, and they just want to work the front counter from time to time and become part of the community. I'd be in charge of billing, the books, ordering and so on."

"Richard, huh?"

A tingle of pleasure skittered down her spine at the jealous note in his voice. Maybe the eight days he'd kept his distance had been the longest in his life, as they had been in hers.

He shook his head. "Something smells fishy."

The *ignoring* part was becoming harder and harder. "With Richard's backing, I can expand the business and offer competitive pricing. We're even designing a Web site where customers can place orders over the Internet. And he's sending two of his store's delivery trucks up from Austin for me to use."

"Sounds too good to be true." His dark eyebrows dipped until they met in the middle of his forehead. "I'll check this Cain fellow out myself."

"No, you won't. I don't want you interfering." She heard the quiet breath he sucked in and regretted the hasty remark.

"Fine." He stormed back to the front of the store.

"Royce, wait!" She scurried past him in the aisle, then skidded to a halt. Pressing her back to the front door, she flung her arms wide, blocking his path. "I want to know why you're so mad. I thought you'd be…happy I'd found a way to save the store."

He focused on the door, not her face. After a moment his gaze met hers and the raw emotion in his eyes caught her off guard. "This is my fault."

"Your fault? What do you mean?"

"I backed off and gave you some space. I thought that after a couple of failures you'd realize selling the business was the smart thing to do. If I'd stepped in right away and taken charge, I could have prevented this ridiculous scheme from ever coming to life."

"It's *not* ridiculous! My decision to take on a partner is a level-headed one. A mature one. I'd hoped you'd see it the same way."

Right then, someone pounded on the front door and the

glass vibrated against her back and shoulders. Jumping, she spotted Fred, standing on the stoop, shaving cream splattered on the front of his shirt, holding a straight-edge razor in one hand. He pointed the razor down the street and frantically gestured.

"What the hell?" Royce moved her aside and opened the door.

"You gotta come quick, Royce. One of the sewer pipes at the end of Main burst. The whole street's flooded."

"Crap," Royce muttered.

"Yep, lots of that running down the sidewalks." Fred scurried away toward the small crowd at the end of the block.

Heather cringed at the dark look Royce sent her before hurrying after the barber. "Wait for me!" She flipped the Open sign in the window to Closed before chasing after the two men. She caught up in seconds, but wished she hadn't. A group of merchants had gathered at the intersection and people were jostling one another for an unrestricted view of the catastrophe.

Royce moved through the crowd and she followed, her stomach threatening to heave as she got her first whiff of the awful stench filling the air. Dirty brown water spewed in a giant geyser from the center of the intersection. The water pressure had blown the manhole off, and Heather thought it a miracle someone hadn't been hurt.

Sheriff Bradson stood in the street, shouting orders to stay clear, while a county truck with barricades stacked in the back pulled around the block. In a matter of minutes the driver had the street closed off.

Heather turned to ask Royce a question, but he'd left her

side. She spotted him several yards away, plugging one ear and holding a cell phone to the other. She couldn't hear the conversation, but the angry flush along his cheekbones made her grateful she wasn't on the other end of the connection.

A moment later, he disconnected the call and searched the crowd. When he saw her, she bit her lip to keep from crying out at the bleakness in his eyes. She hurried toward him and he met her halfway.

"I contacted one of the companies who gave us repair estimates. They'll be here in an hour." He glanced at his watch, then at the foul water in the street. "I have to warn the merchants to check for sewage backing up on their properties. You better keep an eye on the feed store."

To heck with witnesses. She stood on tiptoe and kissed him square on the mouth. She expected a rebuke; instead, he sent her a sad smile of gratitude, which told her just how much this incident upset him. He gave her hand a squeeze, then walked toward the sheriff.

After ten minutes the stench drove the crowds away and the merchants back into their stores. In mute wretchedness, Royce continued to watch the gurgling brown water. Deciding she could do nothing to help, she turned to go and almost plowed into council member Ellen Simms.

"Sorry, I didn't see you." Heather steadied the older woman.

Ellen motioned to the end of the street. "I suspected this would happen."

Chewing on her fingernails, Heather mumbled, "Doesn't look good."

"No. It'll cost a pretty penny to fix. And there's no telling if a temporary repair will last until the whole system can be replaced."

Heather understood the town was a long way from acquiring enough funds to put in a brand-new sewer.

"Oh, before I forget—would you give Royce a message?"

Heather pointed down the street. "He's right over there."

"I see, but I'm not going near him until this mess is cleaned up."

"Don't blame you."

"Tell him the cattle truck won't be at his ranch until Friday. Steward Hansen is stopping in Corpus Christi to pick up a load Thursday. He'll head up here after."

Most ranchers took their cattle to market in the fall. She felt a tingle of suspicion. "How many head is he selling?"

"Every last one."

Oh, no. Her gut told her that Royce had decided to sell his herd in order to come up with the money to repair the town's sewer. She wondered if he had told Luke about his plans. Probably not. She was sure that if Luke had known, the foreman would have protested.

Ellen touched her hand. "I better check my shop and make sure the place doesn't float down the block."

"I'll give Royce the message, Ellen. Talk to you later." Heather couldn't take her eyes off Royce, who was engaged in conversation with a sheriff's deputy at the corner.

She considered how proud he was of this town. How he involved himself in everyone's problems, wanting to help make life in Nowhere fulfilling and purposeful. In her heart she believed he would see this catastrophe as a personal failure.

The fact that he was selling off his herd to help others made Heather want to weep. There had to be a way to pay for the repairs that would allow Royce to keep his cattle. She walked back to the feed store, her mind spinning with ideas.

FOR THE HUNDREDTH TIME, Heather rolled her head to the side and checked the red numbers on the nightstand clock. Three a.m.…and she still hadn't fallen asleep. She sat up and rubbed her swollen, sleep-deprived eyes.

Clad only in panties and a tank top, she left the room and walked to the front of the store. From this vantage point, the torn-up intersection remained out of view. Caution lights flashed an eerie yellow-orange glow against the sides of the buildings farther down the street.

The foul smell of sewage still hung heavy in the air, filtering through every crevice and crack in the store. She'd waited all afternoon and into the night for Royce to stop by and update her on the situation.

At nine p.m. repairs had stopped and the county workers had gone home. She'd continued to wait, but Royce never showed. She'd left the store at about ten and had found him standing in the middle of the dark intersection, studying the gaping hole in the street.

After a few minutes he'd glanced up and made eye contact with her. Then he'd walked away, gotten into his truck and driven off, leaving her to wonder if what they'd shared these past two months had meant anything to him at all.

Leaning her forehead against the warm glass, she closed her eyes and recalled the hours following the disaster. She'd spent most of the time on the phone. She'd offered Richard Cain seventy-five percent of the feed store if he'd help finance a new sewer for the town. The stunned silence before he'd politely turned down the offer told her he thought she'd lost her mind.

But even then, she hadn't given up. She'd made a call to the dean of the Texas A&M science department. After a few inquiries she learned the school didn't have a program that would allow environmental-science students to work in the field, diagnosing and fixing sewer problems. It had been a long shot, but at least she'd tried.

Then she'd toyed with the idea of a county fund-raiser, going as far as contacting merchants of neighboring towns. No one had jumped at the opportunity to donate money to a cause that wouldn't directly benefit their town.

She moved away from the window and wandered through the store aisles. She knew her clientele. Mr. Jones purchased ten bags of corn feed a week, usually on Saturdays. Harold Nichols paid with a different credit card every week. Mrs. Gibbons paid in cashier's checks. And little Billy Waters showed up every Friday afternoon with a note from his mother to purchase a carton of cigarettes for her.

In such a short time she'd integrated herself into this community. And discovered that although she'd left to go to college and find her way in life, the path had led her right back to where she'd started—Nowhere.

And now she didn't want to leave. *Because of Royce.*

She'd been on a mission when she'd stepped off the bus this past June, determined to prove she'd grown into a mature woman, capable of conquering the challenges of saving a failing business. But mostly she'd returned to Nowhere to seek her heart's desire.

Desperately, she yearned for the stubborn rancher to see her as a woman he found worthy of his trust and his love. But she was running out of ideas on how to prove her love for him was the real deal.

Over the past two months, her love for him had evolved, changing in shape, intensity and capacity. Until she'd spent these past weeks with him, she'd never realized all the wonderful qualities he possessed.

Royce gave so unselfishly of himself and his money to others. He put the welfare of his community first, his needs last. His ranch meant the world to him. That he'd sell his livestock to keep from raising the citizens' taxes proved how deeply he cared about the well-being of his neighbors.

And she hadn't forgotten the nasty threat Mrs. Crawford had flung at Royce when the meeting with their lawyers had ended. Without a doubt, Heather believed that unless the preservation society gained possession of Henderson Feed, Mrs. Crawford would do everything in her power to prevent Royce from gaining a seat on the cattlemen's board.

Accustomed to helping others, Royce didn't realize when *he* could use help. Even if she were able to make the man admit it, she doubted he'd ever step forward and ask. *Stubborn fool.*

She wandered back to the counter and sat on the stool, her brain numb from thinking; worse, her body numb from feeling. Royce was not easy on a woman's heart.

She wasn't sure how to convince Royce that her love for him was the grow-old-and-gray-together kind of love and not some young-girl crush. But Royce was afraid to trust her—afraid to trust himself. She understood that only too well.

Returning to her hometown had been one of the hardest things she'd ever done, emotionally. If she'd never come home, though, she'd never have discovered how much she still loved Royce and wanted to be part of his life.

Royce needed to believe that her love for him was true and strong and that she would not wake up one morning in the future and decide that she no longer wanted him because he couldn't give her a child. If it took forever, she'd stick around Nowhere until he learned to trust her.

But first things first. She had a store to take care of.

"WHERE THE HELL is Hansen?" Royce stood in the barn, leaning against Molly's stall, watching Luke pick the dirt from the mare's hoof.

"Did you call him?"

Jeez. He'd lost his frickin' mind. Unable to believe he hadn't thought of the obvious, he counted in his head until he was sure he wouldn't let out a bellow loud enough to blow the roof off the barn.

Since the sewer pipe had broken this past Tuesday, he'd felt like the whole frickin' world had crumbled on top of him and he'd been left buried under a pile of rubble, trying to claw his way out. Normally, he needed all of five minutes to assess a situation and decide on a course of action. But suddenly, his reasoning skills were useless.

"I'll go phone Hansen." Royce ignored the smug grin on Luke's face and headed to the house.

After three attempts, he reached the trucker. "Hansen? Royce McKinnon. It's Friday. Where the hell are you?"

"West of Dallas. Why?"

"Dallas! You're supposed to be here, loading my cattle."

"No, sir. You canceled on me."

"Canceled? The hell I did. Get back here and pick up my beefsteaks." Royce hated the feeling of helplessness that was building inside him.

"Calm down, buddy. Some woman named Heather notified dispatch Wednesday to cancel the pickup."

"Heather canceled?" He'd left town after the sewer disaster without saying goodbye to her because his emotions had been raw. He'd craved one of her smiles, the comfort of her arms. But he hadn't thought he could stop with a simple hug or one of her sympathetic kisses.

"Heather was the name on the message."

What the heck was she up to now? He should have put a tracking device around her ankle the second she stepped off the bus in June. "Sorry I blew up. When can you swing back and get my cows?"

"Middle of next week."

Damn. The people of Nowhere were counting on him to pull off a miracle. He had to have the money from the sale of his cattle to pay for the sewer repairs. The citizens wouldn't be too happy with him if they couldn't flush their toilets pretty soon. He'd never let the town down before, and he didn't intend to start now. "Thanks, Hansen. See you next week."

Royce hung up, then sank onto a kitchen chair. He rubbed his brow, wondering if the headache that had sprung to life Tuesday would ever go away. He'd call the county water department and put a hold on the repairs. And then he'd demand answers—answers only Heather could give him. He grabbed his cell phone from the charger on the counter and left the house.

Once he'd cleared the last cattle guard on the property, he pushed the speed limit, feeling the biting pressure from the invisible demons riding his back. Keeping one eye on the road and one on the phone, he punched in the number for the waste-management supervisor. The man wasn't in, but he got the secretary.

"How can I help you, Mayor?"

"Tell Gunther to put a hold on the sewer repair work. There's been a complication with the financing angle."

"Are you sure, Mr. Mayor? We received a cashier's check for the work yesterday afternoon."

"You what?"

"I said—"

"Who gave you the check?" He clenched the steering wheel, reminding himself not to shoot the messenger.

"Mr. Pulaski from Loyalty Savings and Loan brought the check in."

"Thanks for the information," he grumbled, then cut off the woman's goodbye. He was beginning to feel like a pirate whose crew had just mutinied. He scrolled through his voice-mail messages; and sure enough, late last night when he'd been rounding up the last head of cattle, the bank manager had called and left a message: "Royce. Harold Pulaski. You'll never believe who walked in here today and handed me a check..."

Royce erased the rest of the message. He didn't have to be told who'd walked into the bank with the money. He knew—the sassy blonde with sparkling blue eyes who had landed in town this summer with the force of a nuclear bomb, blowing up everything in her path, including him.

He tossed the phone onto the seat. As he continued to drive, he tried to figure out why Heather would do such a crazy thing when she'd been so set on keeping the store. The fact that she hadn't even consulted him set his britches on fire.

Mrs. Crawford's face flashed before his eyes. Had the older woman contacted Heather again and threatened to keep Royce off the board as a means of intimidating her into selling? His heart felt squeezed at the thought that Heather would sacrifice her store for him and the people of Nowhere.

One way or another, he had to convince her that she didn't have to sell the store. After her struggle to keep it afloat, she deserved a chance to try out the new partnership with the Austin company before she gave up. Besides, he was getting used to Heather's presence in his life. He wasn't ready to let her go...unless—

Then it hit him.

Square between the eyes. Right in the middle of the gut.

As if a twelve-point buck had dropped out of the sky and landed on the hood of the truck, Royce flattened the brake and swerved onto the shoulder. He struggled to get air into his lungs as a cold chill swept through him. How could he have been so dense?

He closed his eyes and rested his head against the wheel. Heather wasn't helping the citizens of Nowhere or him out of the goodness of her heart. Selling the store was her way of saying goodbye.

She'd changed her mind about a future with him. Heather was leaving town and him for good.

His chest felt hot, tight and achy—the pain like nothing he'd ever experienced. Her empty pleas played over and over in his mind. She'd begged him to believe that she loved him. Begged him to believe that it hadn't mattered to her that he couldn't give her children. Begged him to trust her enough to let her into his heart...*damn her!*

Sweat beaded across his brow as he struggled against the constriction in his throat. If there was one thing to be grateful for, it was the fact that he'd been smart enough to hold off baring his soul to her. All this time he'd held his feelings inside, afraid to hope, afraid to believe. Thank God, or he would have looked like a first-class fool.

A deep sadness filled him. Heather was too sweet, too

kind, to tell him face-to-face she'd had second thoughts about a future with him. And he realized exactly how she intended to end things. She'd use the excuse of needing to make arrangements to get her degree as the reason for returning to College Station. After a few days, maybe a week, she'd call to say she'd graduated. The next phone call, maybe a month later, she'd tell him she'd found a great job and she would try to come home for Thanksgiving. Then a holiday card would arrive in the mail, promising that she'd make it back for Christmas. But she wouldn't. Christmas Eve, he'd sit alone in front of the tree, wondering what lucky guy had won Heather's heart. After that holiday, the cards and calls would stop. And then it would be over.

Blast it! If she wanted to end things between them, fine. Easing his foot off the brake, Royce headed into town, determined to make Heather say goodbye face-to-face.

When he pulled into Nowhere, he noticed the construction crew hard at work tearing up the street. A massive blue pipe hung suspended from a crane over the hole in the pavement. A crowd of geriatrics sat in lawn chairs in front of several businesses. Probably the most entertainment the cronies had experienced in a long time.

He swung the truck around the corner, then slowed. Vehicles, parked every which way, jammed the street and a barricade blocked the back lot of the feed store. Outside the building people milled around, while children chased one another up and down the sidewalk. Except for the missing roasted pig, the scene reminded him of a small-town picnic.

He drove farther down the street, searching for a parking space, finding none. He ended up three blocks away and used the long walk back to the store to tamp down his rising anger and hurt.

When he entered the building, he spotted a three-ring circus. And Heather Henderson was the main attraction.

Beautiful and vulnerable, she stood in the center aisle. Surrounded by Mrs. Crawford and her clones, she looked dazed and frazzled. Her teeth worried her lower lip as the editor of the *County Courier* hovered nearby scribbling notes on a writing pad.

Part of him hungered to throw her over his shoulder and steal her away from the chaos. The other part—the frustrated and angry part—wanted to lash out and wound her.

Bunker's nephew rang up purchases at the back counter. He noticed the half-empty shelves, some completely barren. The front display window sported a variety of painted-on messages—Going Out Of Business and Blow-Out Sale. In the far corner in smaller letters, Everything Must Go!

Never taking his eyes off Heather, he maneuvered through the crowd. When she spotted him, her face lost what little color it had had moments ago. The smattering of freckles across her nose stood out like spots on a Dalmatian.

Protectiveness surged through him, but he hardened himself against the feeling. He couldn't remember a time that he hadn't wished to slay all her dragons…he just never expected she'd turn around and slay *him.*

"Excuse me." He bumped the newspaper editor out of the way. "Ms. Henderson and I have urgent business to discuss." He glared pointedly at the people nearby. "In private."

Mrs. Crawford sniffed, then moved away and lost herself among the noisy customers.

Grinding his teeth, he let the words seep out of his mouth. "You owe me an explanation."

Her gaze skidded away from his as if she didn't want to

hurt him with the truth. "This has nothing to do with you, Royce."

"The hell you say!" The racket inside the store quieted to a stunned silence.

Heather flashed an apologetic smile to those around them. Her smile dissolved when she met his gaze. "Can we discuss this later?"

"Might as well have it out right here. Half the town will know the details by sundown."

"Royce, please." She kept glancing at Mrs. Crawford, as if she and the old bat shared some kind of secret. "I'll explain everything. But not here."

He leaned in and whispered, "This isn't about selling the store, Heather."

Her brow puckered in confusion.

"This is about selling out on me…us."

Her faced flushed and she perched her hands on her slim hips. "Selling out? What in the world are you talking about, Royce?"

"You sold the store because you changed your mind about…us."

Eyes flashing, she fired back. "According to you, there never was an *us,* Royce."

Every eyeball in the place was on them. Swallowing against the thickness in his throat he asked, "So this is it? You're leaving? Going back to College Station?"

Her face turned deathly pale. "Is that what you want?"

No! "Yes." There, damn it! He'd said it for both of them.

Tears flooded her eyes and he wondered for one second if he'd made a mistake. *Say something! Tell me I'm wrong. Tell me anything, Heather. Give me a reason to beg you to stay.* Nothing—only silence.

"You still have that bus ticket, don't you?"

"Yes."

"Use it."

A stricken expression came over her face and he had to shift his attention to the back of the store to keep from pulling her into his arms and pleading for forgiveness. "Have a safe trip."

A need to run, anywhere and far away, followed him to the front door. He didn't take a deep breath until he reached the street corner. Determined to find a place to hole up and lick his wounds, he got in his truck and headed out of town for the Timber Shack—a dive known for good whiskey and nothing else.

Chapter Fifteen

Be careful what you wish for.

Royce clenched the empty shot glass, his fingers itching to throw it at the idiot who'd come up with the admonition. He'd parked his butt on a bar stool two hours ago. And all it did was numb his backside—not his mind.

He still hadn't figured out a dang thing about life—no thanks to the bartender. The short, bald man paid more attention to the baseball game on TV than counseling his patrons. Hell, maybe Heather ought to think about tending bar. Lots of opportunities to counsel in a place like this—*except there were no kids.*

He'd already counted the bottles of liquor lined up in rows behind the bar twice, and come up with a different number each time. The acrid smell of sweating bodies, smoke, rank rest rooms and spilled beer disrupted even the most stalwart man's thinking. He should have left the place after the first drink, but he hadn't had the strength to haul his sorry self out of there.

The whiskey bottles blurred before his eyes. He'd wanted Heather to sell the store the day she'd gotten off that bus. Now that she had…well, he should be standing-on-his-head happy, shouldn't he?

He'd taken one look at Heather when she'd stood in the church parking lot that hot, sunny June afternoon and he'd known his heart was in for the fight of its life. She'd scared the hell out of him with her gutsy determination, her spunky attitude and her genuine kindness. He'd tried to convince himself that what he felt for her was mostly sexual.

Nothing like whiskey to make a man admit he'd lied.

"Leave me alone," he muttered, trying to rid his mind of Heather's specter.

"You talkin' to me, pal?"

Royce glanced sideways, wondering why he hadn't noticed the Harley dude sitting next to him. "Sorry." He shook his head. "This is a private conversation."

The guy's bushy gray eyebrows bunched across his forehead. Leather crackled as he slid from the stool and moved to a table in the back corner.

The seat didn't stay empty long. "Mind if I sit a spell?"

At the sound of his foreman's voice, Royce swallowed a groan. The last person he wanted to converse with was the meddling old coot.

"Ain't nothin' worse than a man holed up, lickin' his wounded pride." Luke grinned, his sun-baked skin showing more creases than an outdated road map. "How long you gonna sit here feelin' sorry for yourself?"

"Mind your own business." Royce clenched the shot glass tighter. Maybe if he ignored Luke, the man would take a hike.

The foreman grabbed a fistful of nuts from a bowl on the bar, popped one in his mouth and noisily sucked the salt off the shell. "Ain't sure which one of you is worst for wear."

Well, damn. He couldn't let that comment slide by. "What are you talking about?"

"Stopped by the feed store. That little gal looked so sad and tuckered out you'd think she'd been plowed under by a manure spreader."

Royce's chest tightened with the familiar need to intervene. The urge to drop everything and run to Heather's side—the very thing she'd made clear from the get-go she didn't want or need from him. "She's a big girl. She can take care of herself."

"I suppose she can. But that ain't the point." Luke signaled the barkeep for a draft beer.

"What exactly is the point?"

"She may not need you, but she wants you. Poor gal's sufferin' from lovesickness. Plain as day, even to these ol' cataracted eyes."

Royce's gut twisted at the image of Heather hurting. He didn't want to be the cause of her pain. Besides, Luke had it all wrong. *She* was the cause of *his* pain.

The foreman spat a shell out of his mouth. It landed with a *plop* on the back of Royce's hand. "If you don't love the filly, what's keeping your backside in this dump?"

He figured the old guy wouldn't leave until he spilled his guts. "I do love her, Luke."

A few seconds ticked off. "I know."

"You know?"

"Yep. I figured somethin' had happened between you two after you returned from visitin' her at the university three years ago." A sad expression settled in Luke's eyes. "You should've called her from the hospital, boy. She would've come."

"You think I don't know that?" A flashback of his stay in the hospital sent a sharp pain through his gut. "I didn't want her seeing me flat on my back with bags of ice shoved between my legs. I was so swollen I couldn't even pee on my own!"

"Shush, unless you want everybody hearin' your problems."

Royce lowered his voice. "I didn't want her to see me like that, Luke."

"What about later, after you come home from the hospital. There was three messages from her waitin' on the answerin' machine."

"I couldn't talk to her. Not after learning I was—" He stopped, still amazed how much it hurt to talk about the past.

"You gonna just throw everythin' good in your life away because you're sterile?"

"Didn't throw you away, old man." Luke had been the one to find Royce that terrible night after the attack. The foreman had refused to leave Royce's side at the hospital, sleeping in the chair by the bed. He'd been the one to hug Royce after the doctor had informed him that during the surgery, they'd discovered an absence of vas deferens—a genetic defect in Royce's testes. The tubes that carry sperm from the testes had failed to develop normally, leaving Royce sterile. But the doctor had reassured Royce that the condition would not interfere with normal sexual function.

"Heather phoned a month after I got out of the hospital and I talked to her then. Told her I had second thoughts about us and not to bother coming home for the summer or any other frickin' time after that." He glared. "Satisfied now that you've got the whole story?"

"I'm missin' one part. What'd she say when you told her about the accident."

Royce winced. "I didn't tell her."

Luke gaped. "Why the hell not?"

"Because I didn't want her pity. Didn't want to put her in an awkward position. She would have returned home that summer out of guilt and then…I just couldn't do it, Luke." He snapped his mouth shut when he heard his voice tremble. He hated to admit, even to himself, that right after the accident he'd felt like half a man.

"But you told her you were sterile, didn't you, after things got serious between you two this summer?"

"Yes."

"And?"

"And she said it didn't matter. That she loved me anyway." *She'd lied.*

"Dad blast it, boy! What the hell you sittin' here drinkin' yourself stupid for when the gal that loves your sorry ass is packin' to leave?"

"She sold the store, Luke, don't you get it?"

"Sure I get it. She wanted to help her neighbors out. And I get that she sold the store because she loves you and didn't want you sellin' all your stinky cows. I swear that girl has more sense than you do."

Royce shook his head. "You got it all wrong. Heather's selling out because she's changed her mind and doesn't want to marry a man who can't give her babies."

"She told you that?"

"She didn't have to."

The lines on Luke's face deepened. "I think you got it all wrong, Royce. You're sittin' here on your foolish pride, lettin' the best thing in your life walk away."

"I trusted her. I believed her when she said it didn't matter that I was sterile. I trusted her when she said I was enough to make her happy. Damn it, Luke, I trusted her!"

"Seems to me if anyone needs to do a little trustin' 'round here, it's you learnin' to trust yourself."

"Now, what the hell kind of foolish talk is that?"

"Simple, you dunderhead. If you trust Heather and believe she really loves you, then you have to believe your sterility doesn't matter to her. Which leaves only one person left that hasn't accepted it—you."

"What do you mean?"

Luke poked a finger against Royce's head. "In here, you understand you can't have kids." He moved his finger to Royce's chest. "But in here, you're still grievin'."

"That's the biggest bunch of psychobabble I've ever heard."

"Maybe. Maybe not."

After a minute, Royce asked, "What if she changes her mind and decides five years from now she wants a baby?"

"You just got to trust that she loves you enough to work things out. 'Sides, there's always adoption."

"But she still might leave me." Royce didn't think he'd survive if Heather walked off one day with his heart in tow.

"Life don't give no guarantees. Sometimes love don't never happen for a man. If you're one of the lucky ones and love lands in your lap, grab it and hang on like hell no matter how long it lasts." Luke slid off the stool and started for the door, but stopped mid stride. "In case you're interested. Heather's hoppin' on the next bus out of Nowhere." Without another word he left the bar.

The muscles along the back of Royce's neck tightened. Heather was too young, too full of life and energy to waste time grieving over him. He thought of her married to another man and his gut twisted. *I love her, damn it!* But in so many ways they were opposites.

The spitfire looked on the positive side of things. He considered the negative first. He viewed everything in life as black or white. Heather saw a bit of color in most things. He knew a slew of reasons why they weren't compatible. But none of those reasons had to do with what he felt for her deep down inside. None of those reasons made a difference to his heart.

As long as he was having a discussion with himself he might as well admit he hadn't taken into consideration Heather's best interests when he tried to convince her to sell the store after arriving in Nowhere.

He wanted her gone because he'd felt a yearning for something he feared only she could give him. All these years, he'd lived on the fringes of other people's lives. Always ready to help and guide but never allowing himself to be drawn in deeper.

Standing on the outside was safer—something he'd learned from his aunt and uncle. Anything having to do with love and affection, they'd turned him a cold shoulder. Never a kind word, or even a pat on the back.

When Heather had entered his life this summer, drawing him in with her warm, wacky optimism and generous spirit, he'd begun to want things he'd never thought he needed. No longer were empty words of appreciation enough. He yearned for love. Heather's love…

He closed his eyes and conjured images of her. Watching pretend fireworks on the roof of the feed store. The night he'd snuck inside and caught her working on her college papers. That she hadn't quit school had filled him with great pride. The kiss outside the barn at the barbecue. Her wanton appearance the morning she'd boldly faced the city council members wearing nothing but a sheet.

And finally her sad, tear-filled eyes as he accused her of not loving him because he couldn't give her a child.

*You're a...*meanie, *McKinnon.*

He wasn't good enough for Heather to wipe her sandals on. Even a fool like him could see that any kind of relationship with her had disaster written all over it. After tossing a twenty on the bar, he walked out into the warm August night. He'd always assumed Heather would be the one to leave.

Yet all along, he'd been the one doing the leaving.

THE DAY had started out like any other. The sun rising up, temperatures soaring above ninety degrees by mid morning and people entering and exiting the store. Except this time, they weren't customers. They were repairmen, sent over by the preservation society to begin the restoration process.

Heather sat on the edge of the stripped mattress in the back room, eyeing her suitcases by the door.

Are you sure you want to leave? she asked herself.

What choice did she have? She'd lost the store. She was unemployed. And homeless. Well, okay. Not really homeless. Royce had insisted she could hang her hat at his ranch anytime. But that was just an empty gesture. He wanted her gone from Nowhere. The sooner the better.

Molly. The thought of leaving the ill mare behind made Heather's heart hurt even more. The horse had so little time left and Heather hated that she wouldn't be around to say a final goodbye. Tears burned her eyes but she refused to cry. She'd cried enough over the past forty-eight hours to fill up the hole in the center of Main Street.

If only leaving would stop the pain. Stop her from loving Royce. Time might dull the feeling, although right now she couldn't imagine her love for him mellowing with time, distance or age. But maybe.

Call him.

No. She refused to beg. If the blockhead believed that someday she'd stop loving him because he couldn't give her a baby, then...good riddance!

She'd had enough of not being wanted. Her father had regarded her as nothing more than a responsibility—and one he hadn't wanted. Her mother felt the same way, only she'd flat-out left. Then three years ago her relationship with Royce had changed and for the first time in her life she'd been ready to trust someone with her love. But, like everyone else in her life, Royce had thrown her love right back in her face.

Deep inside she believed Royce did love her in his own way. She'd felt that love in every fiber of her being when they'd been intimate. In the end, though, loving a man who didn't trust her would bring her sorrow, not happiness.

Strong words from a woman whose chest was hollow and aching.

Life had taught Heather one thing. She was a survivor. She'd return to College Station and wallow in self-pity for a while. Maybe a *long* while. Then one morning she'd wake up and the sun would feel warm again on her skin. The cold inside her would recede. When that morning arrived, she'd know for sure she'd be all right. Life would get better. Eventually.

But she feared she'd die before reaching that milestone.

In the meantime she'd have good memories, healing memories of her fight to save the feed store. Of discovering something new about herself—she genuinely *liked* running a business, even the stress and problems that went along with it. Liked setting goals and meeting them. And when the preservation society had challenged her for the building, she'd relished the fight, rising to the task, thriving on the conflict.

Thank goodness the sewer had burst. Blinded by the need to succeed, she'd lost focus on the real reason she'd returned to Nowhere—Royce. Maybe if she hadn't put the feed-store troubles before her relationship with Royce he might have believed her when she said she loved him. She'd messed up royally.

If selling the store was the barrier between her, Royce and a happy-ever-after, she'd stay and fight for him. But she didn't know how to overcome his hang-up about his sterility. Nothing she said made him believe her. Trust her.

Glancing at her watch, she realized the bus would soon pull into town. For the last time, she meandered through the store. The shelves had been disassembled and taken away. Without merchandise, the place really did look like a dump. Peeling paint, cracks in the brick walls, broken floorboards, rusted pipes and stains on the ceiling. Royce had been right. The building needed major renovating, not a few upgrades.

A feeling of rightness settled over her. No way had she been about to stand by and let Royce sell off his herd to help the citizens of Nowhere. All his life, he'd come to the rescue of others, giving unselfishly of his time and money. He might not have accepted her love, but he'd have to accept her gift of money to pay for the sewer repairs. And truthfully, selling the store and paying for the sewer had been the only way Heather could think of to thank the townspeople for the warm, heartfelt welcome they'd given her upon her return. Because of their acceptance, Nowhere would now occupy a fond place in her memory. The preservation society would restore the building to its former glory, and one day, if she had the courage, she'd return to see the changes.

She grabbed her suitcases and left through the back door. Eyes forward, chin high, she walked to the church two blocks away…each step more painful than the last.

Turning the corner, she spotted the large water oak in the church parking lot. The sturdy, gnarled branches spread wide, waiting to enfold her in their shade. When she reached the tree, she set the luggage down and stood one suitcase on its end to use as a seat. While a trio of squirrels played by the bushes, she thought about the things she had to do when she returned to College Station—mainly, find a job.

Before long she heard the gears grind when the bus entered town. As the coach drove into the lot she recognized the driver as the same man who'd brought her here. The bus swung in a wide arc, then came to a stop.

She lifted the suitcases and started across the lot. The driver met her halfway, took the bags and uttered an obligatory "Good afternoon, ma'am."

After he'd stowed the luggage, she handed him the very ticket Royce had offered her that hot, hazy morning a couple of months ago. He gave her the stub back. She had the insane urge to laugh as she studied the torn half of the ticket—a memento for her scrapbook.

"We're almost full up. There're two seats left in the back."

"Thank you." She stepped onto the bus, and the scent of cloying perfume, exhaust fumes and stale body odor drifted past her nose. *Oh, joy.*

The two remaining seats were located on either side of the toilet. Neither travel companion looked desirable. She bypassed the rumpled man leering at her from behind a newspaper and slid onto the cushion next to a pimply faced, greasy haired high school kid playing a computer game that bleeped every few seconds.

A moment later the driver boarded and shut the door. He scribbled something in a notebook, then shifted gear and eased up on the brake. The bus was rolling out of the lot when the sound of a blaring horn caught the driver's attention. The coach rocked to a jarring stop.

Turning in her seat, Heather glanced out the window. Her breath caught. Then her heart stalled before resuming a painful pounding rhythm.

A black Dodge sped up the block. It squealed to a stop directly in front of the parking lot exit.

Heather forced herself to stay calm. "Excuse me," she mumbled, then all but shoved the teenager out of the way as she scrambled closer to the window. Royce got out of the truck and stared up at the bus. *He's searching for you, Heather.*

She held her breath, afraid to consider why he'd blocked the exit. A moment later, she exhaled loudly as he moved around the hood of the truck. Scowling, the bus driver reached for the handle and opened the door.

Royce climbed inside and paused at the front, ignoring the driver's mumbled protest. He looked so handsome in tight jeans, a pearl-snap western shirt and his Stetson.

Except for a few appreciative female murmurs, the passengers remained silent. In slow motion he removed his shades, then scanned the seats from front to back.

Heather bit her lip to keep from calling out his name and

waving *Here I am!* Finally, his gaze landed on her, and the heat in his eyes sent her stomach into a somersault. She doubted there would ever be another man who could melt her down with just a look the way Royce McKinnon could. Not in this lifetime, anyway.

The corner of his lip lifted. "Goin' somewhere, Heather?"

Shivers of something that she was afraid to label but that was awfully close to hope shimmied down her spine as the question carried to the back. Afraid that if she answered, the word would come out sounding like a squawk, she nodded.

His eyes pinned her to the seat. "You don't listen too well, do you." He moved forward one step. The tension on the bus tightened a notch. "I thought I told you to stay put."

Stunned, she could say nothing, but the tight band around her heart loosened with each passing second. She tried to recall their conversation eight weeks ago when he'd met her as she'd gotten off this very same bus. Holding back a smile, she taunted, "You ought to know by now, that I don't listen too well."

He took another step forward. "Seems to me you need someone to keep you in line."

Hope turned to joy. "Depends."

He continued toward her until he stood two seats away. At this distance, she could see the dark circles under his eyes. The mayor looked as if he'd lost his best friend. "Depends on what?"

"Not what. *Who.*"

He broke eye contact for a moment. When his gaze returned to her face, she felt the world tilt. She blinked, but the bright sheen in his eyes was still there. Her own filled with moisture.

He pinched the bridge of his nose and inhaled deeply. "I thought I could do it, but I can't."

Leaning forward in her seat, she whispered, "Can't what?"

"Let you go."

Feeling as if she teetered on the edge of a cliff, she called on every ounce of control she possessed to stay seated and let the man have his say.

His brown eyes churned with emotion. "You blew into town, all fired up and determined to grab the world by the toes, upsetting everything and everyone in your path—including me." He moved forward and crouched on his heels in front of her.

Lord have mercy, Royce McKinnon was on his knees!

Her heart started the climb back to her chest, one hopeful inch at a time. She clasped his hand in hers and allowed him to see in her eyes all the love she felt for him.

"Jeez, man. Just tell the chick, already, will ya?" The kid next to Heather grumbled.

Royce smiled, a full from-the-heart grin.

If she hadn't already been sitting, she'd have fallen on her fanny.

"I'm not letting you leave, Heather."

She gasped, fighting the tears wobbling on the ends of her lashes.

"It wasn't you I didn't trust, Heather. It was me. Please forgive me and say it's not too late for us. I love you more than anything in this world."

He stood, and she rocketed out of the seat, launching herself against him. The clanging of her heart almost drowned out the cheering bus passengers. Burrowing her nose against Royce's warm neck, she inhaled his familiar musky aftershave, which she'd come to love so dearly.

"I'll stay, but only on two conditions," she murmured against his flesh.

He raised her chin. "And they are…?"

"That you promise me you'll never doubt my feelings for you."

"Done."

"That we get married right away. I don't want to give you time to change your mind."

"Done."

Amid the good wishes of the passengers, Royce carried her off the bus, then set her on the ground outside and kissed the breath out of her. The kiss went on forever, and neither was aware the driver had unloaded Heather's bags, then backed the bus up and exited the parking lot. All that surrounded her was Royce, his warmth. His *love.*

She could have stood kissing him until sunset, but she had to be sure about one more thing. "Do you believe me when I say that it doesn't matter that you can't give me a baby? That I'll never stop loving you because of that?"

He leaned his forehead against hers. "I do. I think I believed you when you first said so, but I was scared."

"If I do want that baby someday, are you open to adoption?"

"Yeah. I'd like us to have a family together. You'd make a great mother."

"Good. Because you'd make a great father." She snuggled against his chest. "There are so many children who need someone to love them, someone to care what happens to them."

"We'll find those children, Heather, and we'll love them. Together."

"C'mon, cowboy. Take me home. We have some loving

of our own to catch up on before our life gets complicated with a bunch of rugrats."

Royce pressed a gentle kiss to her lips. "Kids or no kids, loving you will always come first in my heart."

Hand in hand, Royce and Heather headed for the truck, and their very own happily-ever-after in Nowhere land.

Welcome to the world of American Romance!
Turn the page for excerpts from our
September 2005 titles.
We're sure you'll enjoy every one of these books!

It's time for some BLOND JUSTICE!
Downtown Debutante is Kara Lennox's
second book in her series about three women
who were duped by the same con man and
vow to get revenge.
We know you're going to love this
fast-paced, humorous story!

Brenna Thompson drew herself deeper into the down comforter, trying to reclaim the blessed relief of sleep. But instead of drifting off again, she awoke with a jolt and smacked into hard reality. She was stranded in Cottonwood, Texas, without a dime to her name, her entire future hanging by a thread.

And someone was banging on her door at the Kountry Kozy Bed & Breakfast.

Wearing only a teddy, she slid out of bed and stumbled to the door. "I told you to take the key," she said grumpily, opening the door, expecting to see Cindy, her new roommate. "What time is it, any—" She stopped as her bleary eyes struggled to focus. Standing in the hallway was a broad-shouldered man in a dark suit, a blindingly white shirt and a shimmering blue silk tie. He was a foot taller than Brenna's own five-foot-three, and she had to strain her neck to meet his cool, blue-eyed gaze.

In a purely instinctual gesture, she slammed the door closed. My God, she was almost naked. A stranger in a suit had seen her almost naked. Her whole body flushed, then broke out in goose bumps.

The knock came again, louder this time.

"Uh, just a minute!" She didn't have a robe. She wasn't a robe-wearing sort of person. But she spied one belonging to Sonya, her other roommate, lying at the foot of her bed. The white silk garment trailed the floor, the sleeves hanging almost to Brenna's fingertips—Sonya was tall—but at least it covered her, sort of.

Taking a deep breath, she opened the door again. "Yes?"

Still there. Still just as tall, just as imposing, just as handsome. Not her type, she thought quickly. But there was a certain commanding presence about this stranger that made her stomach swoop and her palms itch.

"Brenna Thompson?"

Deep voice. It made all her hair follicles stand at attention.

"Yes, that's me." He didn't smile, and a frisson of alarm zapped through her. "Is something wrong? Oh, my God, did something happen to someone in my family?"

He hesitated. "No. I'm Special Agent Heath Packer with the FBI. This is Special Agent Pete LaJolla."

Brenna saw a second man lurking in the shadows. He stepped closer and grunted a greeting. Both men looked as if they expected to enter.

Brenna glanced over her shoulder. The room was a complete wreck. Every available surface was covered with clothes and girly stuff, not to mention baby things belonging to Cindy's little boy. Even fastidious Sonya's bed was unmade. Sonya was used to servants doing that sort of thing for her.

Special Agent No. 1 didn't wait for her consent. He eased past her into the room, his observant gaze taking everything in.

"If you'd given me some warning, I could have tidied up," she groused, pulling the robe more tightly around her. She hadn't realized how thin the fabric was.

Mustering her manners, Brenna cleared off a cosmetics case and a pair of shoes from the room's only chair. "Here, sit down. You're making me nervous. And…Agent La-Jolla, was it?" She brushed some clothes off Sonya's twin bed. LaJolla nodded and sat gingerly on the bed while Brenna retreated to her own bed. She sat cross-legged on it, drawing the covers over her legs both for warmth and modesty.

"I assume you know why we're here," Packer said.

If you enjoyed Penny McCusker's first book
for American Romance,
MAD ABOUT MAX (April 2005),
you'll be happy to hear that her second book,
NOAH AND THE STORK, has arrived!
And if you haven't read her before,
you'll be delighted by Penny's warmhearted humor
in this charming story set in the town
of Erskine, Montana.

Men were generally a pain in the neck, Janey Walters thought, but there were times when they came in handy. Like when your house needed a paint job, or your kitchen floor needed refinishing or your car was being powered by what sounded like a drunk tap dancer with a thirst for motor oil.

Or when you woke in the middle of the night, alone and aching for something that went way beyond physical, into realms best left to Hallmark and American Greetings. Whoever wrote those cards managed to say everything about love in a line or two. Janey didn't even like to think about the subject anymore. Thinking about it made her yearn, yearning made her hopeful, and hope, considering her track record with the opposite sex, was a waste of energy.

She set her paintbrush on top of the can and climbed to her feet. She'd been sitting on the front porch for the past hour, slapping paint on the railings, wondering if the petty violence of it might help exorcise the sense of futility that had settled over her of late. All she'd managed to do was polka-dot everything in the vicinity—the lawn and rose bushes, the porch floor and herself—which only made more work for her and did nothing to solve the real problems.

And boy, did she have problems. No more than any other single mom who lived in a house that was a century old, with barely enough money to keep up with what absolutely had to be fixed, never mind preventative maintenance. And thankfully, Jessie was a normal nine-year-old girl—at least she seemed well-adjusted, despite the fact that her father had never been, and probably would never be, a part of her life.

It only seemed worse to Janey now that her best friend had gotten married. But then, Sara had been waiting for six years for Max to figure out he loved her, and Janey would never have wished for a different outcome. She and Sara still worked together, and talked nearly every day, so it wasn't as if anything had really changed in Janey's life. It just felt…emptier somehow.

She put both hands on the small of her aching back and stretched, letting her head fall back and breathed deeply, in and out, until she felt some of the frustration and loneliness begin to fade away.

"Now there's a sight for sore eyes."

Janey gasped, straightening so fast she all but gave herself whiplash. That voice… Heat moved through her, but the cold chill that snaked down her spine won hands down. It couldn't be him, she told herself. He couldn't simply show up at her house with no warning, no time to prepare.

"The best scenery in town was always on this street."

She peeked over her shoulder, and the snappy comebacks she was famous for deserted her. So did the unsnappy comebacks and all the questions she should've been asking. She couldn't have strung a coherent sentence together if the moment had come with subtitles. She was too busy staring at the man standing on the other side of her wrought-iron fence.

His voice had changed some; it was deeper, with a gravelly edge that seemed to rasp along her nerve endings. But there was no mistaking that face, not when it had haunted her memories—good and bad—for more than a decade. "Noah Bryant," Janey muttered, giving him a nice, slow once-over.

Tina Leonard continues her popular COWBOYS BY THE DOZEN series with Crockett's Seduction. These books are wonderfully entertaining and exciting. If you've never read Tina Leonard, you're in for a treat. After all, who can resist a cowboy—let alone twelve of them! Meet the brothers of Malfunction Junction and let the roundup of those Jefferson bad boys begin!

Even now, at his brother Bandera's wedding, Crockett Jefferson wondered if Valentine Cakes—the mother of his brother Last's child—realized how much time he spent staring at her. His deepest, darkest secret was that she evoked fantasies in his mind, fantasies of the two of them—

"Well, that's that," his eldest brother, Mason, said to Hawk and Jellyfish, the amateur detectives and family friends who'd come to the Malfunction Junction ranch to deliver news about Maverick Jefferson, the Jefferson brothers' missing father.

Before he heard anything else, Crockett once again found his eyes glued to Valentine and her tiny daughter, Annette. Watching her was a habit he didn't want to give up, no matter how much family drama flowed around him.

Hawk looked at Mason. "Do you want to know what we learned about your father before or after you eat your piece of wedding cake?"

Crockett sighed, and took a last look at the fiery little redhead as he heard the pronouncement about Maverick. She was holding her daughter and a box of heart-shaped petits fours she'd made for Bandera's wedding reception. She smiled at him, her pretty blue eyes encouraging, her mouth bowing sweetly, and his heart turned over. With regret he looked away.

She could never know how he felt about her.

He really didn't *want* to feel the way he did about the mother of his brother's child. So, to get away from the temptation to keep staring, he followed Hawk, Jellyfish and Mason under a tree so they could talk.

"We were able to confirm that Maverick was in Alaska, for a very long time," Hawk said.

Crockett thought Mason surely had to be feeling the same excitement and relief that filled him; finally some trace of Maverick had been found.

"But we felt it was important to come back and tell you the news, then let you decide what more you need to learn," Hawk said.

Crockett felt a deep tug in his chest. Now they would hold a family council to decide what to do. It was good they'd found out now, since all the brothers were at the ranch for the annual Fourth of July gathering and Bandera's wedding.

Now that so many of the Jefferson brothers had married and moved away, Mason wanted to hold a family reunion at least twice a year—Christmas in the winter and Fourth of July in the summer. Christmas was a natural choice, but Independence Day was a time when the pond was warm enough for the children to swim, Mason had said. But Crockett knew his request really had nothing to do with pond water. Mason just wanted the brothers and their families together, on the so-called Malfunction Junction ranch, their home.

Crockett had to admit there was something to the power of family bonding as he turned to again watch Valentine with her tiny daughter.

His Wedding, by Muriel Jensen,
is Muriel's last book in the saga of
the Abbotts, a northeastern U.S. family
whose wealth and privilege could not shield
them from the harsher realities of life,
including a kidnapping. At last the mystery of the kid-
napping is solved—by the missing Abigail herself, with
the help of Brian Girard, himself an Abbott child who is
soon planning his wedding!

Brian Girard sat on the top porch step of his shop at just after 6:00 a.m., drinking a cup of coffee while reading the *Losthampton Leader*. The ham-and-cheese bagel he'd bought tasted like sawdust when he saw the front-page article about Janet Grant-Abbott's move to Losthampton, and he'd thrown the bagel into the garbage.

"Long-lost heiress home again," said the caption under a photo of Janet that must have been taken on her return from Los Angeles.

From the small plane visible some distance behind her, the setting was obviously the airport. Her hair was short and fluffy, and she was squinting against the sun.

At a glance she resembled any other young woman on a casual afternoon. It was the second look that made you realize she was someone special. Her good breeding showed in the tilt of her head and the set of her shoulders; the intellect in her eyes elevated a simple prettiness to fascinating beauty.

The article revealed all the known details of her kidnap, the Abbott family's position in the world of business, her brothers' accomplishments, then her own history as a successful stockbroker.

It went on to say that her adopted sister had come to Losthampton thinking she might be the missing Abbott sister, Abigail, but that a DNA test had proven she wasn't. And that had brought Janet onto the scene.

He was just about to give the reporter credit for a job not-too-badly done, when he got to the part about himself:

"Brian Girard, the illegitimate son of Susannah Steward Abbott, Nathan Abbott's first wife, and Corbin Girard, the Abbotts' neighbor, has been welcomed into the bosom of the family." It continued in praise of their generosity, considering that Corbin Girard was responsible for the fire in their home and the vandalism to the business Brian owned. It explained in detail that Brian had been legally disowned for defecting to the Abbott camp by giving the Abbotts information that stopped them from making a business deal they would have regretted. Brian has no idea how the paper had gotten that information, unless one of the family had told them.

Annoyed, he threw the newspaper in the trash, on top of the bagel, and strode, coffee cup in hand, down his dock. The two dozen boats he'd worked so hard to repair bobbed at the ends of their lines, a testament to his determination to start over at something he enjoyed.

The refinished shop was restocked with the old standbys people came in for day after day, plus a few new gourmet products, a line of sophisticated souvenirs and shirts and hats with his logo on them—a rowboat with a grocery bag in the bow—visible proof of his spirit to survive in the face of his father's continued hatred.

He could fight all the roadblocks in his path, he thought, gazing out at the sun rising to embroider the water with light, but how could he fight the truth? No matter what he did, he would always be the son of a woman who'd thrown away her husband and other two sons like so much outdated material, and of a man who'd rejected him since the day he was born.

The sorry fact was that Brian couldn't fight it. He could do his best to be honest and honorable, but he would never inspire a favorable newspaper article. Every time his name came up, it would be as the son of his reprehensible parents.

He didn't know what to do about it.

Then again, Janet Grant-Abbott wasn't sure what to do, either.

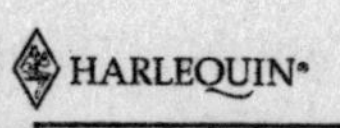

Fatherhood

Fatherhood: what really defines a man.

It's the one thing all women admire in a man—
a willingness to be responsible for a child and
to care for that child with tenderness and love.

NOAH AND THE STORK
by Penny McCusker

September 2005

Noah Bryant's job has brought him back to Erskine, Montana—and the girl he once loved. It's no surprise that Janey Walters is all grown up now with a daughter of her own. But Noah gets the shock of his life when he finds out he's Jessie's father….

BREAKFAST WITH SANTA
by Pamela Browning

November 2005

Tom Collyer unwillingly agrees to fill in as Santa at the annual Farish, Texas, Breakfast with Santa pancake fest. He's not surprised by the children's requests for the newest toys. He is surprised when one young boy asks for something Tom—or Santa—can't promise to deliver: a live-in father.

Available wherever Harlequin Books are sold.

www.eHarlequin.com HARFH0805